PAN'S LABYRINTH

THE LABYRINTH OF THE FAUN

GUILLERMO del TORO

CORNELIA FUNKE

ILLUSTRATIONS BY ALLEN WILLIAMS

KATHERINE TEGEN BOOKS
An Imprint of HarperCollins Publishers

Katherine Tegen Books is an imprint of HarperCollins Publishers.

Pan's Labyrinth: The Labyrinth of the Faun

Library of Congress Cataloging-in-Publication Data

Names: Toro, Guillermo del, 1964– author. | Funke, Cornelia, 1958- author. | Young adult novelization of (work): Toro, Guillermo del, 1964- Laberinto del fauno (Motion picture)
Title: Pan's labyrinth : the labyrinth of the faun / Guillermo del Toro and Cornelia Funke.
Other titles: Labyrinth of the faun
Description: First edition. | New York, NY : Katherine Tegen Books, an imprint of HarperCollinsPublishers, [2019]
Identifiers: LCCN 2018034307 | ISBN 978-0-06-241446-5 (hardback)
Classification: LCC PZ7.1.T629 Pan 2019 | DDC [Fic]—dc23 LC record available at https://lccn.loc.gov/2018034307

Typography by Joel Tippie
19 20 21 22 23 PC/LSCH 10 9 8 7 6 5 4 3 2 1

First Edition

For Alfonso Fuentes and his men, who saved my house, my trees, my donkeys,

my memories, and my notebooks from the Woolsey Fire

—C.F.

For K, the solution to all the riddles, the way out of the Labyrinth

—G.D.T.

CONTENTS

PROLOGUE

It is said that long, long ago, there lived a princess in an underground realm, where neither lies nor pain exist, who dreamt of the human world. Princess Moanna dreamt of a perfect blue sky and an infinite sea of clouds; she dreamt of the sun and the grass and the taste of rain. . . . So, one day the princess escaped her guards and came to our world. Soon the sun erased all her memories and she forgot who she was or where she came from. She wandered the earth, suffering cold, sickness, and pain. And finally, she died.

Her father, the king, would not give up searching for her. For he knew Moanna's spirit to be immortal and hoped that it one day would come

back to him.

In another body, at another time. Perhaps in another place.

He would wait.

Down to his last breath.

Until the end of time.

1

The Forest and the Fairy

There once was a forest in the north of Spain, so old that it could tell stories long past and forgotten by men. The trees anchored so deeply in the moss-covered soil they laced the bones of the dead with their roots while their branches reached for the stars.

So many things lost, the leaves were murmuring as three black cars came driving down the unpaved road that cut through fern and moss.

But all things lost can be found again, the trees whispered.

It was the year 1944 and the girl sitting in one of the cars, next to her pregnant mother, didn't understand what the trees whispered. Her name was Ofelia and she knew everything about the pain of loss, although she was only thirteen years old. Her father had died just a year ago and Ofelia missed him so terribly that at times her heart felt like an empty box with nothing but the echo of her pain in it. She often wondered whether her mother felt the same, but she couldn't find the answer in her pale face.

"As white as snow, as red as blood, as black as coal," Ofelia's father used to say when he looked at her mother, his voice soft with tenderness. "You look so much like her, Ofelia." Lost.

They had been driving for hours, farther and farther away from everything Ofelia knew, deeper and deeper into this never-ending forest, to meet the man her mother had chosen to be Ofelia's new father. Ofelia called him the Wolf, and she didn't want to think about him. But even the trees seemed to whisper his name.

The only piece of home Ofelia had been able to take with her were some of her books. She closed her fingers firmly around the one on her lap, caressing the cover. When she opened the book, the white pages were so bright against the shadows that filled the forest and the words they offered granted shelter and comfort. The letters were like footprints in the snow, a wide white landscape untouched by pain, unharmed by memories too dark to keep, too sweet to let go of.

"Why did you bring all these books, Ofelia? We'll be in the country!" The car ride had paled her mother's face even more. The car ride and the baby she was carrying. She grabbed the book from Ofelia's hands and all the comforting words fell silent.

"You are too old for fairy tales, Ofelia! You need to start looking at the world!"

Her mother's voice was like a broken bell. Ofelia couldn't remember her ever sounding like that when her father was still alive.

"Oh, we'll be late!" Her mother sighed, pressing her handkerchief to her lips. "He will not like that."

He . . .

She moaned and Ofelia leaned forward to grab the driver's shoulder.

"Stop!" she called. "Stop the car. Don't you see? My mother is sick."

The driver throttled the engine with a grunt. Wolves—that's what they were, these soldiers accompanying them. Man-eating wolves. Her mother said fairy tales didn't have anything to do with the world, but Ofelia knew better. They had taught her everything about it.

She climbed out of the car while her mother stumbled to the side of the road and vomited into the ferns. They grew as densely between the trees as an ocean of feathery fronds, from which gray-barked trunks emerged like creatures reaching up from a sunken world below.

The two other cars had stopped as well and the forest was swarming with gray uniforms. The trees didn't like them. Ofelia could sense it. Serrano, the commanding officer, came to check on her mother. He was a tall, bulky man who talked too loudly and wore his uniform like a theater costume. Her mother asked him for water in her broken-bell voice, and Ofelia walked a little way down the unpaved road.

Water, the trees whispered. *Earth. Sun.*

The fern fronds brushed Ofelia's dress like green fingers, and she lowered her gaze when she stepped on a stone. It was gray like the soldiers' uniforms, placed in the middle of the road as if someone had lost it there. Her mother was once again vomiting behind her. Why does it make women sick to bring children into the world?

Ofelia bent down and closed her fingers around the stone. Time had covered it in moss, but when Ofelia brushed it off, she saw it was flat and smooth and that someone had carved an eye on it.

A human eye.

Ofelia looked around.

All she could see were three withered stone columns, almost invisible among the high ferns. The gray rock from which they were carved was covered with strange concentric patterns and the central column had an ancient corroded stone face gazing out into the forest. Ofelia couldn't resist. She stepped off the road and walked toward it, although her shoes were wet with dew after just a few steps and thistles clung to her dress.

The face was missing an eye. Just like a puzzle missing a piece—waiting to be solved.

Ofelia gripped the eye-stone and stepped closer.

Underneath the nose chiseled with straight lines into the gray surface, a gaping mouth showed withered teeth. Ofelia stumbled back, when between them a winged body as thin as a twig stirred, pointing its long, quivering tentacles at her. Insect legs emerged from the mouth and the creature, bigger than Ofelia's hand, hastily scuttled up the column. Once it reached the

4

top, it raised its spindly front legs and started gesturing at her. It made Ofelia smile. It seemed like such a long time since she'd last smiled. Her lips weren't used to it anymore.

"Who are you?" she whispered.

The creature waved its front legs once more and uttered a few melodic clicking sounds. Maybe it was a cricket. Did crickets look like this? Or was it a dragonfly? Ofelia wasn't sure. She had been raised in a city, between walls built from stones that had neither eyes nor faces. Nor gaping mouths.

"Ofelia!"

The creature spread its wings. Ofelia followed it with her eyes as it flew away. Her mother was standing just a few steps down the road, Officer Serrano by her side.

"Look at your shoes!" her mother chided with that soft resignation her voice held so often now.

Ofelia looked down. Her damp shoes were covered with mud, but she still felt the smile on her lips.

"I think I saw a Fairy!" she said. Yes. That's what the creature was. Ofelia was sure.

But her mother wouldn't listen. Her name was Carmen Cardoso, she was thirty-two years old and already a widow and she didn't remember how it felt to look at anything without despising it, without being afraid of it. All she saw was a world that took what she loved and ground it to dust between its teeth. So as Carmen Cardoso loved her daughter, loved her very much, she had married again. This world was ruled by men—her child didn't understand that yet—and only a man would be able to keep them both safe. Ofelia's mother didn't know it, but she also believed in a fairy tale. Carmen Cardoso believed the most dangerous tale of all: the one of the prince who would save her.

The winged creature that had been waiting for Ofelia in the column's gaping mouth knew all of this. She knew many things, but she was not a Fairy—at least not in the sense we like to think of them. Only her master knew her true name, for in the Magic Kingdom to know a name was to own the being that carried it.

From the branch of a fir tree, she watched Ofelia and her mother get back into the car to continue their journey. She'd waited for this girl for a long time: this girl who had lost so much and would have to lose so much more to find what was rightfully hers. It wouldn't be easy to help her, but that was the task her master had given her, and he didn't take it lightly when his orders weren't followed. Oh no, he didn't.

Deeper and deeper into the forest the cars drove, with the girl and the mother and the unborn child. And the creature Ofelia had named a Fairy spread her insect wings, folded her six spindly legs, and followed the caravan.

ALL THE SHAPES EVIL TAKES

Evil seldom takes shape immediately. It is often little more than a whisper at first. A glance. A betrayal. But then it grows and takes root, still invisible, unnoticed. Only fairy tales give evil a proper shape. The big bad wolves, the evil kings, the demons, and devils . . .

Ofelia knew that the man she would soon have to call "Father" was evil. He had the smile of the cyclops Ojancanu and the cruelty of the monsters Cuegle and Nuberu nesting in his dark eyes, creatures she had met in her fairy-tale books. But her mother didn't see his true shape. People often grow blind when they get older and maybe Carmen Cardoso didn't notice the wolfish smile because Capitán Vidal was handsome and always

7

impeccably dressed in his gala uniform, boots, and gloves. Because she wished so badly for protection, maybe her mother mistook his bloodlust for power and his brutality for strength.

Capitán Vidal looked at his pocket watch. The glass face was marred by a crack, but the hands underneath still told the time and they indicated that the caravan was late.

"Fifteen minutes," muttered Vidal, who, like all monsters—like Death—was always punctual.

Yes, they were late, just as Carmen had feared, when they finally arrived at the old mill Vidal had chosen to serve as his headquarters. Vidal hated the forest. He hated everything that didn't keep a proper order, and the trees were far too willing to hide the men he had come here to hunt. They fought the very darkness Vidal served and admired, and he had come to the old forest to break them. Oh yes, Ofelia's new father loved to break the bones of all those he considered weak, to spill their blood, and give new order to their messy, miserable world.

He greeted the caravan. Smiling.

But Ofelia saw the contempt in his eyes as he welcomed them in the dusty yard where once upon a time, peasants of the surrounding villages had delivered their grain to the miller. Her mother, though, smiled at him and allowed the Wolf to touch her belly swollen with his child. She even gave in when he told her to sit in a wheelchair like a broken doll. Ofelia watched it all from the backseat of the car, despising the prospect of offering the Wolf her hand as her mother had told her to. But finally she climbed out, to not leave her mother alone with him, pressing her books against her chest like a shield made from paper and words.

"Ofelia." The Wolf crunched her name between his thin lips into something as broken as her mother, and stared at her extended left hand.

"It's the other hand, Ofelia," he said softly. "Remember."

He was wearing black leather gloves that creaked when he enclosed Ofelia's hand in a grip as fierce as a poacher's trap. Then he turned his back on her, as if he'd already forgotten about her.

"Mercedes!" he called out to a woman who was helping the soldiers unload the cars. "Get their luggage!"

Mercedes was slim and pale. She had raven-black hair and dark liquid eyes. Ofelia thought she looked like a princess pretending to be a peasant's daughter. Or perhaps an enchantress, though Ofelia wasn't sure which kind, good or evil.

Mercedes and the men carried her mother's suitcases to the mill house. Ofelia thought it looked lost and sad, as if it missed being a mill grinding fresh grain. Now it was overrun with soldiers, swarming around its withered stone walls like locusts. Their tents and trucks were everywhere, filling the wide yard surrounded by stables, a barn, and the mill itself.

Gray uniforms, a sad, old house, and a forest filled with shadows . . . Ofelia yearned to go home so badly she could barely breathe. But there was no home without her father. She felt tears welling up behind her eyes, when she suddenly noticed between sacks stacked a few feet away a pair of wings catching the sunlight as though made of paper-thin glass.

It was the Fairy.

Forgetting her sadness, Ofelia ran after her, when she made a beeline for the trees behind the mill. The little creature was so fast that Ofelia soon stumbled over her own feet as she chased her, dropping all her books. But when Ofelia picked them up, wiping the dirt from their covers, she saw the Fairy clinging to the bark of a nearby tree, waiting for her.

She was. Oh yes. She had to make sure the girl followed her.

But wait. No! She had halted her steps again.

Ofelia was staring at a huge arch that had appeared between the trees, spanning the gap between two ancient walls. A horned head stared down from the arch with empty eyes and an open mouth, as if it were trying to swallow the world. The gaze of those eyes seemed to make everything vanish: the mill, the soldiers, the Wolf, even Ofelia's mother. *Come in!* the crumbling walls seemed to say. Ofelia could see faded engraved letters below the head but she didn't know their meaning.

In consiliis nostris fatum nostrum est, the words read.

"In our choices lie our fate."

The Fairy had disappeared, and when Ofelia stepped through the arch, it cast a cold shadow on her skin. *Turn around!* something in her warned. But she didn't. Sometimes it is good to listen, sometimes it is not. Ofelia wasn't sure she had a choice anyway. Her feet did the walking all by themselves. The corridor that opened behind the arch narrowed after just a few steps until Ofelia could touch the walls on either side simply by stretching out her arms. She dragged her hands over the withered stones while she kept walking. They were so cold despite the heat of the day. A few more steps and she reached a corner. Another corridor opened in front of her, leading left and then right toward another corner.

"It is a labyrinth."

Ofelia spun around.

Mercedes was standing behind her. The shawl draped across her shoulders looked as if she had woven it from woolen leaves. If she was an enchantress, she was a beautiful one, not old and withered as they mostly looked in Ofelia's books. But she knew from the tales that enchantresses often didn't wear their true faces.

"It's just a pile of old stones," Mercedes said. "Very old. Older than the mill. These walls have been here forever—long before the mill was built. You shouldn't come in here. You could get lost. It has happened before. I'll tell you the story one day if you want to hear it."

"Mercedes! The *capitán* needs you!" a soldier's harsh voice ordered from behind the mill.

"I'm coming!" Mercedes called back.

She smiled at Ofelia. There were secrets in her smile, but Ofelia liked her. She liked her very much.

"You heard that. Your father needs me." Mercedes started walking back to the arch.

"He is not my father!" Ofelia called after her. "He is *not*!"

Mercedes slowed.

Ofelia ran to her side and they walked through the arch,

leaving the cold stones and the horned face with the empty eyes behind.

"My father was a tailor," Ofelia said. "He was killed in the war."

There were the tears again. They always came when Ofelia talked about him. She couldn't help it.

"He made my dress and the blouse my mother wears. He made the most beautiful clothes. More beautiful than the princesses wear in my books! Capitán Vidal is *not* my father."

"You've made that very clear," Mercedes said gently, putting her arm around Ofelia's shoulders. "But come now. I'll take you to your mother. I'm sure she's already looking for you."

Her arm felt warm. And strong.

"Isn't my mother beautiful?" Ofelia asked. "It is the baby who makes her sick. Do you have a brother?"

"I do," Mercedes replied. "You'll see, you will love your little brother. Very much. You won't be able to help it."

She smiled once again. There was sadness in her eyes. Ofelia saw it. Mercedes seemed to know about losing things too.

Sitting atop the stone arch, the Fairy watched them walk back to the mill: the woman and the girl, spring and summer, side by side.

The girl would come back.

The Fairy would make sure of that.

Very soon.

As soon as her master wished.

3

JUST A MOUSE

Yes, Mercedes had a brother. Pedro was one of the men hiding in the forest, a Maqui, as they called themselves, a resistance fighter, hiding from the very soldiers Mercedes cooked and cleaned for.

Capitán Vidal and his officers were planning the hunt for those men when Mercedes walked in with the bread, cheese, and wine he had ordered. At one time the table on which they'd spread their map used to serve meals to the miller and his family. Now all it served was death. Death and fear.

The flames dancing in the fireplace painted shadows of knifes and rifles onto the whitewashed walls and the faces bending over the map. Mercedes put her tray down and cast an unsuspicious glance at the marked army positions.

13

"The guerrillas stick to the forest because it's hard to track them there." Vidal's voice was as expressionless as his face. "The scum knows the terrain much better than we do. We'll therefore block all access to the woods. Here. And here." He brought his black-gloved finger down on the map like a missile.

Pay attention, Mercedes. And tell your brother what they are planning, or he'll be dead in a week.

"Food, medicine, we'll store it all. Right here." Vidal pointed at the spot that marked the mill. "We need to force them down from the hills. That way they'll come to us."

Here, Mercedes. They'll store it all here!

She took her time laying the food out on the table, glad that she was completely invisible to them, just a maid, just part of the room like the chairs and the firewood.

"We'll set up three new command posts. Here, here, and here."

Vidal placed bronze markers on the map. Mercedes didn't take her eyes off his gloved fingers. That's what she was: the eyes and ears of the rabbits they hunted, as silent and invisible as a mouse.

"Mercedes!"

She forgot to breathe when the black glove grabbed her shoulder.

Vidal's eyes were narrow with suspicion. *He is always suspicious, Mercedes,* she thought, calming her racing heart. He liked to watch his gaze spread fear on a face, but she'd played this game often enough to not give herself away. Just a mouse. Invisible. She'd be done for if he ever came to believe that she was a cat or a vixen.

"Ask Dr. Ferreira to come down."

"Yes, *señor.*"

She bent her head to make herself small. Most men didn't want a woman to be tall. Vidal was no exception.

Three command posts. And food and medicine stored at the mill.

Now *that* would come in handy.

A Rose on a Dark Mountain

Dr. Ferreira was a good man, a gentle soul. That much was apparent to Ofelia the moment he walked into her mother's room. One can spot kindness as clearly as cruelty. It spreads light and warmth and the doctor seemed filled with both.

"This will help you sleep," he told her mother as he added a few drops of amber liquid to a glass of water.

Her mother hadn't argued with him when he advised her to stay in bed for a few days. It was a huge wooden bed, with plenty of room for her and Ofelia to share. Her mother hadn't been well at all since they'd come to this miserable place. Her forehead was wet with sweat, and pain etched fine

16

lines into her beautiful face. Ofelia was worried, but it comforted her to watch the doctor's calm hands prepare the draught.

"Just two drops," he said, handing Ofelia the small brown bottle so she could close it. "You'll see it will help her."

Her mother could barely swallow the water without gagging.

"You need to drink all of it," Dr. Ferreira softly urged. "Very good."

His voice was as warm as the blankets on the bed and Ofelia wondered why her mother hadn't fallen in love with a man like the doctor. He reminded her of her late father. Just a little bit.

Ofelia had just sat down on the side of the bed, when Mercedes came into the room.

"He wants you downstairs," she said to Dr. Ferreira.

He. Nobody spoke his name. Vidal. It sounded like a stone thrown through a window, each letter a piece of broken glass. Capitán. That's what most of them called him. But Ofelia still thought Wolf fit him much better.

"Don't hesitate to call me," the doctor said to her mother as he closed his bag. "Day or night. You or your young nurse," he added, smiling at Ofelia.

Then he left with Mercedes, and Ofelia was alone for the first time with her mother in this old house smelling of cold winters and the sadness of people from ages past. She liked to be alone with her mother. She always had, but then the Wolf had come.

Her mother drew her closer.

"My young nurse." She pushed her hand under Ofelia's arm with a tired but happy smile. "Close the doors and turn off the light, *cariño*."

Even though she'd be at her mother's side, Ofelia dreaded the prospect of sleeping in this strange room, but she did as she was told. She was reaching for the door latch, when she saw the doctor standing on the landing with Mercedes. They didn't notice her and Ofelia didn't want to eavesdrop, but she couldn't help listening. To listen . . . after all, that's what being a child is about. Learning about adults' secrets means learning to understand their world—and how to survive it.

"You have to help us, Doctor!" Mercedes was whispering. "Come with me and see him. The wound's not healing. His leg is getting worse."

"This is all I could get," the doctor said quietly, handing Mercedes a small parcel wrapped in brown paper. "I am sorry."

Mercedes took the parcel, but the despair on her face frightened Ofelia. Mercedes seemed so strong, like someone who would protect her in this house filled with loneliness and the ghosts of the past.

"The *capitán* is waiting for you in his office." Mercedes straightened her back and didn't look at Dr. Ferreira as he descended the stairs. His steps were heavy, as if he felt guilty walking away from Mercedes's desperate face.

Ofelia couldn't move.

Secrets. They add to the darkness of the world but they also make you want to find out more. . . .

Ofelia was still standing by the open door when Mercedes turned. Her eyes widened with fear the moment she saw Ofelia and she hastily hid the parcel under her shawl, while Ofelia's feet finally obeyed and she stepped back to latch the door, wishing Mercedes would just forget she had seen her.

"Ofelia! Come here!" her mother called from the bed.

At least the fire spread some light in the dark room, along with two flickering candles on the mantelpiece. Ofelia crawled into the bed and wrapped her arms around her mother.

Just the two of them. Why hadn't that been enough? But her baby brother was already kicking in her mother's belly. What if he was like his father? *Go away!* Ofelia thought. *Leave us alone. We don't need you. For she has me and I take care of her.*

"Heavens, your feet . . . they're frozen!" her mother said.

Her body felt so warm. Maybe a bit too warm, but the doctor hadn't seemed too worried about the fever.

Around them the mill was moaning and creaking. It didn't want them. It wanted the miller back. Or maybe it wished to be alone with the forest, tree roots breaking through its walls, leaves covering its roof, until its stones and beams became part of the forest again.

"Are you afraid?" her mother whispered.

"A little," Ofelia whispered back.

Another moan rose from the old walls, and the beams above them sighed as if someone was bending them. Ofelia pressed closer against her mother. She kissed Ofelia's hair, as black as her own.

"It's nothing, *cariño*. It's nothing, just the wind. Nights are very different here. In the city you hear cars, the tramway. Here the houses are so much older. They creak. . . ."

Yes, they did. This time they both listened.

"It sounds as if the walls are speaking, doesn't it?" Her mother hadn't held Ofelia like this since she had learned she was pregnant. "Tomorrow. Tomorrow I'm giving you a surprise."

"A surprise?" Ofelia looked up at her mother's pale face.

"Yes."

Ofelia felt so safe in her embrace. For the first time since . . . since when? Since her father died. Since her mother met the Wolf.

"Is it a book?" she asked. Her father had often given her books. Sometimes he had even tailored clothes for them. *Linen. To protect the binding, Ofelia,* he would say. *They bind them in very cheap fabric nowadays. This is better.* Ofelia missed him so much. Sometimes it felt as if her heart were bleeding and it wouldn't heal until she saw him again.

"A book?" Her mother laughed softly. "No! Not a book! Something much better."

Ofelia didn't remind her mother that for her, there was nothing better than a book. Her mother wouldn't understand. She didn't make books her shelter or allow them to take her to another world. She could only see this world, and then, Ofelia thought, only sometimes. It was part of her mother's sadness to be earthbound. Books could have told her so much about this world and about places far away, about animals and plants, about the stars! They could be windows and doors, paper wings to help her fly away. Maybe her mother had just forgotten how to fly. Or maybe she'd never learned.

Carmen had closed her eyes. At least when she was dreaming she saw more than this world, didn't she? Ofelia wondered, pressing her cheek against her mother's chest. So close, their bodies fusing into one, as they had been before she was born. Ofelia could hear the tide of her mother's breath, the soft thumping of her heart beating so regularly, like a metronome against bone.

"Why did you have to get married?" Ofelia whispered.

As the words escaped her lips, part of her hoped that her mother was already asleep. But then the answer came—

"I was alone for too long, my love," her mother said, staring at the ceiling above them. The whitewash was cracked and lined with spiderwebs.

"But *I* was with you!" Ofelia said. "You were not alone. I was *always* with you."

Her mother continued to stare at the ceiling, suddenly seeming so far away. "When you're older you'll understand. It wasn't easy for me, either, when your father—"

She drew in her breath sharply and pressed her hand on her swollen belly. "Your brother is acting up again."

Her mother's hand felt so hot when Ofelia covered it with her own. Yes, she could feel her brother too. And no, he wouldn't go away. He wanted to come out.

"Tell him one of your stories!" her mother gasped. "I am sure that'll calm him down."

Ofelia felt reluctant to share her stories with him, but finally she sat up.

Under the white sheets her mother's body looked like a mountain covered in snow, her brother sleeping in its deepest cave. Ofelia put her head on the bump in the blanket, caressing it where her brother was moving, deep under her mother's skin.

"Brother!" she whispered. "Brother of mine."

Her mother hadn't given him a name yet. He would need one soon to get ready for this world.

"Many, many years ago . . . in a sad, faraway land . . ." Ofelia spoke in a soft, low voice, but she was sure he could hear her. "There was an enormous mountain made of black flint . . ."

Behind the mill, in the forest as dark and silent as the night, the creature Ofelia called the Fairy spread her wings and followed the sound of the girl's voice, the words building a path of bread crumbs through the night.

"And atop that mountain," Ofelia continued, "a magic rose blossomed every dawn. People said whoever plucked it would become immortal. But no one dared to go near it because its thorns were filled with poison."

Oh yes, there are many roses like that, the Fairy thought as she flew toward the window behind which the girl was telling her story. When she slipped into the room, her wings fluttering as softly as Ofelia's voice, she saw them: the girl and her mother, holding each other against the darkness of the night outside. But the darkness inside the house was far more frightening, and

22

the girl knew that it was fed by the man who'd brought them here.

"People talked about all the pain the thorns of the rose could cause," Ofelia whispered to her unborn brother. "They warned each other that whoever climbed the mountain would die. It was so easy for them to believe in the pain and the thorns. Fear helped them believe that. But none of them dared to hope that in the end the rose would reward them with eternal life. They couldn't hope—they could not. And so, the rose would wilt away, night after night, unable to bequeath its gift to anyone. . . ."

The Fairy sat on the windowsill to listen. She was glad the girl knew about the thorns, as she and her mother had come to a very dark mountain. The man who ruled this mountain—oh yes, the Fairy knew all about him—was sitting downstairs in his office, the room behind the mill's wheel, polishing the pocket watch of his father, another father who had died in another war.

"The rose was forgotten and lost," Ofelia said, pressing her cheek to her mother's belly. "At the top of that cold, dark mountain, forever alone until the end of time."

She didn't know it, but she was telling her brother about his father.

5

FATHERS AND SONS

Vidal cleaned his father's pocket watch every night, the only time when he took off his gloves. The room Vidal had made his office was the one right behind the huge wheel that had once helped grind the miller's corn. Its massive spokes covered most of the back wall and at times gave him the feeling of living inside the watch, which was strangely comforting. He polished the richly engraved silver casing and brushed the dust off the gearwheels as tenderly as if he were caring for a living thing.

Sometimes the objects we hold dear give away who we are even more than the people we love. The glass of the watch had cracked in the hand of Vidal's father at the very moment he died, which his son took as proof that things could survive death if only one kept them clean and in perfect order.

24

His father was a hero. Vidal had grown up with that thought. He had built himself around it. A true man. And that thought brought a memory, almost invariably, of the day when he and his father had visited the cliffs of Villanueva. The rugged seascape on the horizon, the jagged rocks beneath—a hundred-foot drop. His father had gently guided him to the edge and then held him fast. He had grabbed his son when he recoiled, forcing him to look down into the abyss. "Feel that fear?" his father asked. "You must never forget it. That is what you must feel every time you grow weak—when you try to forget that you serve your fatherland and your station in life. When you are faced with death or honor. If you betray your country, your name, or your heritage, it will be as if you take a step forward to take a plunge. The abyss is invisible to you, but it is no less real. Never forget it, my son. . . ."

A knock on the door made the present delete the past. It was a knock so soft that it betrayed who was asking for permission to enter.

Vidal frowned. He hated anything interrupting his nightly ritual. "Come in!" he called, keeping his attention on the shiny workings of the watch.

"Capitán."

Dr. Ferreira's steps were as soft and careful as his voice. He stopped a short distance from the table.

"How is she?" Vidal asked.

The wheels of the pocket watch began to move in their perfect rhythm, confirming once again that there was no end to well-kept order. Immortality was clean and precise. For sure it didn't need a heart.

A heartbeat became irregular so easily and at the end it stopped, however carefully one treated it.

"She is very weak," Dr. Ferreira said.

Yes, soft. That's what the good doctor was. Soft clothes, soft voice, soft eyes. Vidal was sure, he could have broken him as effortlessly as he could a rabbit's neck.

"She'll get as much rest as she needs," he said. "I'll sleep down here."

That would make things easier anyway. He had grown tired of Carmen. He grew tired of every woman quite easily. They usually tried to get too close. Vidal didn't want anyone to get close. It made him vulnerable. All order was lost when love moved in. Even desire could be confusing unless one fed it and moved on. Women didn't understand that.

"And what about my son?" he asked. The child was all he cared about. A man was mortal without a son.

The doctor looked at him in surprise. His eyes always looked slightly surprised behind those silver-rimmed glasses. He opened his soft mouth to answer when Garces and Serrano appeared in the doorway.

"Capitán!"

Vidal silenced his officers with a wave of his hand. The fear on their faces never ceased to please him. It even made him forget what a miserable place this was, so far away from the cities and battlefields where history was written. Being stationed in this dirty, rebel-infested forest—he would make it count. He would plant fear and death with such precision that the generals who had sent him here would hear about it. Some of them had fought with his father.

"My son!" he repeated, impatience cutting like a razor in his voice. "How is he?"

Ferreira still looked at him with bewilderment. *Did I ever meet a man like you?* his eyes seemed to ask. "For the moment," he replied, "there is no reason to be alarmed."

Vidal reached for a cigarette and his cap. "Very good," he said, pushing his chair back. Which meant: *Go.*

But the doctor was still standing in front of the table.

"Your wife shouldn't have traveled, Capitán. Not at such a late state of pregnancy."

What a fool. A sheep shouldn't talk like that to a wolf.

"Is that your opinion?"

"My professional opinion. Yes, Capitán, it is."

Vidal slowly walked around the table, his uniform cap under his arm. He was taller than Ferreira. Of course. Ferreira was a small man. He was losing his hair and his scraggly beard made him look old and pathetic. Vidal loved the clean-shaven chin a sharp razor delivered. He felt nothing but contempt for men like Ferreira. Who wants to heal in a world that is all about killing?

"A son," he stated calmly, "should be born wherever his father is."

Fool. Vidal walked toward the door, the smoke of his cigarette following him through the sparsely lit room. Vidal didn't like lights. He liked to see his own darkness. He was almost at the door when Ferreira once again raised his annoyingly gentle voice.

"What makes you so sure the baby is male, Capitán?"

27

Vidal turned with a smile, his eyes as black as soot. He could make men feel his knife between their ribs just by looking at them.

"You should leave," he said.

He could see that Ferreira felt the blade.

~･↓～

The soldiers on guard duty had captured two rabbit hunters poaching past the curfew. Vidal was surprised that Garces had found that worth calling him, although all his officers knew how much he hated to be disturbed at such a late hour.

The moon was a starved sickle in the sky when they stepped out of the mill.

"At eight we detected movement in the northwest sector," Garces reported as they crossed the yard. "Gunfire. Sergeant Bayona searched the area and captured the suspects." Garces always talked as if he were dictating his words.

The captives, one old and one much younger, were as pale as the sickly moon. Their clothes were filthy from the woods and their eyes were dim with guilt and fear.

"Capitán," the younger one said as Vidal scrutinized them wordlessly, "this is my father." He gestured to the older man. "He is an honorable man."

"I'll be the judge of that." Although Vidal enjoyed fear in a man's face, it made him angry at the same time.

"And uncover your head in front of an officer."

The son removed his worn-out cap. Vidal knew why the boy was avoiding

28

his eyes. Dirty peasant! He was proud—one could hear it in his voice—and clever enough to know that his captors wouldn't like that.

"We found this on them." Serrano handed Vidal an old rifle. "It's been fired."

"We were hunting for rabbits!" The boy was proud and without respect.

"Did I say you could talk?"

The old man was so scared that his knees almost gave way. Scared for his son. One of the soldiers holding him yanked the rucksack from his bent shoulders and handed it to Vidal. He pulled out a pocket almanac issued by the Republican government to all farmers—it looked like it had been read many times. The back cover showed the Republican flag and Vidal read the slogan aloud with a sneer:

"'No god, no country, no master.' I see."

"Red propaganda, Capitán!" Serrano looked proud and relieved that he hadn't just disturbed his *capitán* for two dirty peasants. Maybe these two even belonged to the resistance fighters against General Franco, who they had come to hunt in this accursed forest.

"It's *not* propaganda!" the son protested.

"Shhh."

The soldiers heard the threat in Vidal's hissed warning, but the stupid young peacock was too eager to protect his father. Love kills in many ways.

"It's just an old almanac, Capitán!"

No, the boy wouldn't shut up.

"We are just farmers," his father said, trying to draw Vidal's gaze from his son.

"Go on." Vidal liked it when they started pleading for their lives.

"I went up into the woods to hunt rabbits. For my daughters. They are both sick."

Vidal sniffed at a bottle he drew out of the old man's rucksack. Water. One had to do these things calmly to enjoy them.

Order. Even in these things.

"Rabbits . . . ," he said. "Really?"

He knew the son would step into the trap. Oh yes, he knew how to do this. The generals shouldn't have wasted his talents in this forest. He could have done great things.

"Capitán, respectfully," the son said, "if my father says he was hunting rabbits, he was hunting rabbits." He hid his pride under his lowered lids, but his lips betrayed him.

Calmly. That's how it had to be done.

Vidal took the bottle of water and slammed it into the young peacock's face. Then he drove the shattered glass into his eye. Again and again. *Let the rage have its way or it will consume you.* The glass cut and smashed, turning skin and flesh into bloody pulp.

The father screamed louder than the son, tears painting smears onto his dirty cheeks.

"You killed him! You killed him! Murderer!"

Vidal shot him in the chest. It was not much of a chest. The bullets found his heart easily. Two bullets through his dirty, ragged clothes and cardboard bones.

The son was still moving, his hands red with his own blood as he pressed them against the gaping wounds on his face. What a mess. Vidal shot him, too. Under the pale sickle of the moon.

The forest was watching as silently as his soldiers.

Vidal wiped his gloved hands clean on the rucksack, then upended it onto the ground. Papers. More papers. And two dead rabbits. He held them up. They were scrawny little things, mere bones and fur. Maybe a stew would have come out of them.

"Maybe next time you'll learn to search these assholes properly," he said to Serrano, "before you come knocking at my door."

"Yes, Capitán."

How stiffly they all stood there.

What? Vidal challenged them with his eyes. He had a temper. Yes. What were they thinking now, staring at the two dead men at their feet? That some of their fathers and brothers were peasants too? That they also loved their daughters and their sons? That one day he would do the same to them?

Maybe.

We are all wolves, he wanted to say to them. *Learn from me.*

THE SCULPTOR'S PROMISE

Once upon a time, there was a young sculptor named Cintolo. He served a king in a realm so far underground that neither the sun's beams nor the moonlight could find it. He filled the royal gardens with flowers sculpted from rubies and fountains sculpted from malachite. He carved busts of the king and queen that were so lifelike, everyone believed they could hear them breathe.

Their only daughter, the princess Moanna, loved to watch the sculptor work, but Cintolo never managed to sculpt her form. "I can't sit still for that long, Cintolo," she said. "There's too much to do and too much to see."

Then one day Moanna was gone. And Cintolo remembered how often she'd asked him about the sun and the moon and whether he knew what the trees, whose roots laced the ceiling of her bedroom, looked like above the ground.

The king and queen were so heartbroken that the Underground Kingdom echoed with their sighs, and their tears covered the sculptor's flowers like dew. The Faun, who advised them on all affairs of beasts and the sacred things breathing underground, sent out his messengers—bats and fairies, rabbits and ravens—to bring Moanna back, but all those eyes were unable to find her.

The princess had been gone for 330 years when one night the Faun walked into Cintolo's workshop, where the sculptor had fallen asleep amid his tools. He longed to comfort Their Majesties by chiseling Moanna's countenance from a beautiful moonstone, but as hard as he tried, he couldn't remember the princess's face.

"I have a task for you, Cintolo," said the Faun, "and you won't be allowed to fail. I want numerous sculptures of the king and queen—as numerous as the uncurling fronds of ferns—to grow from the soil in the Upper Kingdom. Can you make them?"

Cintolo wasn't sure, but no one dared to say no to the Faun, as he was known for his temper and his influence on the king. So Cintolo went to work. One year later, hundreds of stone columns grew out of the Upper Kingdom's soil, wearing the sad faces of Moanna's parents, carrying the Faun's hope that the lost princess might one day walk past them and be reminded of who she was. But once again, many years passed and there was no news of Moanna. Hope died in the Underground Kingdom like a flower bereft of rain.

Cintolo grew old, but he couldn't bear the thought that he might die before his skills had helped to bring his royal masters' lost child back. So he asked for an audience with the Faun.

The Faun was feeding the swarm of fairies that served him, when the sculptor walked in. The Faun fed them with his tears to remind them of Moanna, as fairies tend to be quite forgetful creatures.

"Your Horned Highness," the sculptor said, "may I offer my humble skills one more time to find our lost princess?"

"And how do you intend to do that?" the Faun asked as the fairies licked another tear from his clawed fingers.

"Please allow me not to answer your question," Cintolo said. "I don't know yet whether my hands will be able to create what I see in my mind. I hope, though, that despite my silence you will agree to sit for me so I may sculpt you."

"Me?" The Faun was surprised by Cintolo's request. But in the old man's face he saw passion, patience, and the most valuable virtue of all in desperate times: hope. So he dismissed all other duties—of which the Faun had many—to sit patiently for the sculptor.

Cintolo didn't use stone for this sculpture. He carved the Faun's likeness from wood, for wood always remembers it was once a living tree, alive and breathing in both kingdoms, the one above and the one below.

It took Cintolo three days and three nights to finish the sculpture and, when he told the Faun to rise from his chair, so did his wooden image.

"Tell it to find her, Your Horned Highness," the sculptor said. "I promise it will neither rest nor die before he does."

The Faun smiled, for he noticed another rare quality in the old man's face: faith. Faith in his art and in what it could do. And for the first time in many years the Faun dared to hope again.

But there are many roads in the Upper Kingdom and, although the sculptor's creature walked through forests and deserts and crossed plains and mountains, it couldn't find the lost princess and fulfill its creator's promise. Cintolo was devastated, and when Death knocked at his workshop door, he didn't send Her away, but followed Her, hoping to forget his failure in the land of oblivion.

Cintolo's creature felt his death like a sharp pain. Its wooden body, aged and weathered by wind and rain and all the miles it had traveled in its search, stiffened with sadness and its feet wouldn't take another step. Two columns rose from the ferns lining the path it had followed. They wore the sad faces of the king and queen, for whose daughter it had searched in vain for so long. Determined to fulfill its quest, the creature plucked out its right eye and laid it on the forest path. Then it walked stiffly into the ferns and turned to stone next to the king and queen it had failed, its mouth open in a last petrified sigh.

The eye, forever bearing witness to the old sculptor's skills, lay on the wet ground for countless days and nights. Until one afternoon three black cars came driving through the forest. They stopped under the old trees and a girl climbed out. She walked down the path until she stepped on the eye Cintolo had carved. She picked it up and looked around to see from where it might have come. She saw the three weathered columns, but didn't recognize the faces they wore. Too many years had passed.

But she did notice one of the columns was missing an eye. So she walked through the ferns until she was standing in front of the column that had once been Cintolo's wooden faun. The eye from the path fit perfectly into the hole that gaped in the weather-beaten face and at that moment, in a chamber so deep underneath the girl's feet only the tallest trees could reach it with their roots, the Faun raised his head.

"Finally!" he whispered.

He picked a ruby flower from the royal gardens to lay on Cintolo's grave and sent one of his fairies up to find the girl.

6

INTO THE LABYRINTH

Ofelia woke to the sound of fluttering wings. A dry, chitinous rustle: angry, brief, then the rattling of something moving in the dark. The candles and the fire had burned down. It was so cold.

"Mother!" Ofelia whispered. "Wake up! There's something in the room."

But her mother wouldn't wake. Dr. Ferreira's drops had given her a sleep as deep as a well and Ofelia sat up shivering, although she still wore her woolen sweater over her nightgown, listening. . . .

There!

Now it was right above her! Ofelia pushed the blankets aside to switch on the light, but she hastily drew her legs back into the bed when she felt something brush against her.

And then she saw her.

The insect Fairy was sitting atop the footboard, her long antennae quivering, her spindly front legs gesturing, her mouth chirping softly in a language that, Ofelia was sure, came straight out of the stories in her books. She held her breath as the winged creature climbed down the bed frame and scampered over the blanket on her stiff legs. She crossed the vast field of wool to finally stop barely a foot away from Ofelia, who noticed with surprise that all her fear had vanished. Yes, it was gone! All she felt was happiness, as if an old friend had found her in this cold, dark room.

"Hello!" she whispered. "Did you follow me?"

The antennae twitched and the strange clicking sounds her visitor made reminded Ofelia of her father's sewing machine and of his needle softly tapping against a button he was attaching to a new dress for her doll.

"You are a Fairy, right?"

Her visitor seemed to not be sure.

"Wait!" Ofelia took one of her fairy-tale books from the bedside table and flipped through to find the page that showed the black cut-paper silhouette she'd looked at so often.

"Here!" She turned the open book to her visitor. "See? That's a Fairy."

Well. If the girl thought so. Ofelia's visitor decided to play along. She raised herself to her hind legs and, turning her back on the girl, lost her antennae and made her dry, elongated body resemble the tiny woman in the illustration. In transforming herself, she gave her wings a slightly different shape. She made them resemble leaves. Then she raised her now-human hands and, brushing her pointed ears with her newly grown fingers,

39

compared her silhouette one more time with the illustration. Yes. The metamorphosis had been successful. Actually, this body might prove to be a new favorite, although she'd taken many shapes in her immortal life. Change was in her nature. It was part of her magic and her favorite game.

But now it was time to fulfill the task for which she'd been sent to the mill. She fluttered toward the girl with her new wings and addressed her with vehemence. *Come along!* she gestured, giving her signal all the urgency her master's orders demanded. He wasn't the most patient one.

"You want me to follow you? Outside? Where?"

So many questions. Humans asked them about everything, but they usually weren't half as good at finding the answers. The Fairy fluttered toward the door. The leaf wings worked really well, but she had her doubts about the body. The insect limbs had been much lighter and faster.

It mattered none. Her master was waiting.

There was still no fear in Ofelia's heart when she slipped into her shoes and followed the Fairy out of the house into the night. It almost felt as if she'd followed her before, and who wouldn't trust a Fairy, even when she showed up in the middle of the night? They probably always did. And you had to follow them. That's what the books said, and didn't their tales feel so much truer than what adults pretended this world to be about? Only books talked about all the things adults didn't want you to ask about—Life. Death. Good and Evil. And what else truly mattered in life.

Ofelia was not surprised when the stone arch surged from the darkness.

The Fairy swirled through it. Mercedes was not at Ofelia's side to stop her, not this time. The labyrinth's ancient stone walls loomed to her left and right, leading her farther and farther into endless circles, and each time Ofelia hesitated at a corner, the Fairy urged her on. *Follow me! Follow me!* Ofelia was sure that was what she chirped, fluttering sometimes high above her, sometimes right by her side.

How long had she been walking? Ofelia couldn't tell. The ancient walls framed the night sky and her shoes were soaked with dew from the moss that carpeted the twisting passages. It all felt like a dream, and there is no time in dreams. Suddenly the walls widened and Ofelia walked into a large courtyard. At the center a huge stone well opened in the ground. There was a staircase leading into it. Ofelia couldn't tell how many steps there were; it seemed to be infinite—the darkness swallowed them all. A whisper of dank air surged from the well pit and Ofelia again felt the pang of fear, but also the call for adventure.

She followed the Fairy, who was twittering and swirling ahead, down the steps, deeper and deeper underground. The stairs ended at the bottom of the well, but there was no water, just a sculpted monolith similar to the ones she'd seen in the forest. It looked equally ancient, but this one was much taller and surrounded by stone canals carved deep into the floor that formed a labyrinth mirroring the one above. There was a rustle in the shadows behind the monolith, as if something big was moving there, and Ofelia was by now quite frightened but the Fairy was still urging her on. Finally, she followed her down the last few steps and stood at the bottom of the well.

"Hello?" Ofelia called. "Hello!"

She thought she heard the sound of rushing water as her own steps echoed up the well.

"Echo!" she called, while the Fairy was swirling around the column. "Echoooo!" to chase the silence away.

The Fairy had landed on a dead tree trunk. Or so it seemed. But when the winged creature touched its gnarled surface with her hands, it shuddered and what Ofelia had thought to be the bent remains of an old tree stirred, straightened, and—turned around.

Whatever it was, it was huge, as were the bent horns on its bulky head. The face that scrutinized Ofelia with catlike eyes was unlike any she'd ever seen. A goat beard covered its chin while cheeks and forehead showed the same ornaments that were carved on the column, and when the creature ripped itself free from the web of moss and dry vines that melded it to the wall, Ofelia saw that its body was half man and half goat. Insects and trapped earth fell from its hide and its bones cracked when it moved its limbs as if it had stood in the shadows for too long.

"Ah! It's you!" he exclaimed. Yes, Ofelia was sure it was a he. "You have returned!"

The creature took a tentative clumsy step toward Ofelia, spreading his pale, clawed fingers like roots. He was indeed huge, much taller than a man, his hoofed legs resembling the hind legs of a goat. His eyes, though shaped like a cat's, were blue, a pale blue, like stolen pieces of sky, with pupils nearly invisible while his skin looked like splintered bark, overgrown, as if he'd been down here for centuries, waiting. . . .

The Fairy was twittering with pride. She'd delivered the girl, as her master had ordered.

"Look! Look who your sister brought!" he purred, opening the wooden satchel he wore strapped across his torso.

Out fluttered two Fairies in the same shape their sister had copied from the pages of a book. Their horned master chuckled with delight when they all swirled around Ofelia, who was clutching her sweater more firmly over her nightgown in the cold, wet air that filled the well. No wonder the Fairies' master moved so stiffly. Though maybe he was just old. He looked old. Very old.

"My name is Ofelia," she said, trying her best to sound brave and not intimidated at all by the horns and those strange blue eyes. "Who are you?"

"Me?" The creature pointed at his withered chest. "Ha!" He waved his hand, as if names were the least important thing in the world. "Some call me Pan. But I've had so many names!" He took a few stiff steps. "Old names that only the wind and the trees can pronounce . . ."

He disappeared behind the monolith, but Ofelia could still hear his voice, a hoarse, mesmerizing rasp of a voice.

"I am the mountain, the woods, and the earth. I am . . . arrghh . . ." He bleated not unlike a goat, looking very old and very young at the same time, when he appeared in front of her once again. "I am"—he shook his limbs with the growl of an aged ram—"a Faun! And I am, as I always was and always will be, your most humble servant, Your Highness."

Ofelia was lost for words, when cracking with effort, he lowered his horned head and addressed her with a deep bow. *Your Highness?* Oh no. He

43

mistook her for somebody else! Of course. She should have known! Why should a Fairy come to her? She was just a tailor's daughter.

"No!" she finally managed to say, backing away. "No, I . . ."

The Faun raised his head and straightened his stiff back.

"You are Princess Moanna. . . ."

"No, no!" Ofelia protested. "I am—"

"The daughter of the king of the Underworld," the Faun interrupted.

What was he talking about? His words scared Ofelia more than the night or this place so far away from the bed warmed by her mother's body. Although we may wish for it, true magic is a scary thing.

"No! No!" she protested once more. "My name is Ofelia. My mother is a seamstress and my father was a tailor. You have to believe me."

Ofelia felt the Faun's impatience when he firmly shook his horned head, but she could also detect a trace of amusement in his patterned face.

"Nonsense, Your Highness. You"—he pointed his clawed finger at her—"were not born from a human womb. The moon gave birth to you."

The Fairies vigorously nodded their small heads. A beam of moonlight made its way down into the well pit, as if it too wished to add proof to the Faun's statement, and lined the wings of the Fairies with silver.

"Look at your left shoulder," the Faun said. "You'll find a mark that proves what I say."

Ofelia gazed at her left shoulder, but she didn't dare to push back her clothes to expose her skin. She wasn't sure what she feared more: that the Faun spoke the truth or that he lied.

A princess!

"Your real father had us open portals all over the world to allow you to return. This is the last one." The Faun gestured at the chamber they were standing in. "But before you are allowed back in his kingdom we have to make sure your essence is intact and you haven't become a mortal. To prove that . . ." He once again reached into his satchel. "You must complete three tasks before the moon is full."

The book he pulled out of the satchel seemed far too big to ever have fit in there. It was bound in brown leather.

"This is the *Book of Crossroads*," the Faun said while handing the heavy book to Ofelia. The lines on his forehead swirled like patterns drawn by wind and waves. "Open it only when you're alone. . . ."

The small pouch he gave her next rattled when Ofelia shook it, but the Faun didn't tell her what to do with it. He just watched her with his pale blue eyes.

"The book will show you your future," he said, stepping back into the shadows. "And what must be done."

The book was so big that Ofelia could barely hold it. It nearly slipped out of her hands when she finally managed to open it.

The pages she was looking at were empty.

"There's nothing written in it!" she said.

But when she looked up, the Faun was gone and so were the Fairies. There was only the night sky above her and the pattern of the labyrinth at her feet.

7

RAZOR TEETH

Vidal's razor was a wondrous thing with its shining blade, sharper than the teeth of a wolf. It had an ivory handle and the steel was German-made. He had taken it from the window of a looted store in Barcelona. A high-end store of gentlemen's articles: travel kits, grooming kits, pipes, pens, and tortoiseshell combs. But to Vidal this razor had never been just a grooming tool. It was a tool that allowed a man to slash and bite. The razor was his claw—his teeth.

Men were such vulnerable creatures, no fur, no scales to protect their soft flesh. So Vidal took great care every morning to turn himself into a more dangerous beast. When the razor swiped his cheeks and chin its

46

sharpness became part of him. In fact, Vidal liked to imagine it turned his heart, scrape by scrape, into metal. He loved to watch how the blade gave his face the order and shine this place of exile was lacking. He wouldn't rest until this dirty forest was like the clean-shaven face he saw in the mirror each time the razor had done its work.

Order. Strength. And a nice metal shine. Yes, that's what he would bring to this place. Blades cut both trees and men so easily.

After he'd taken care of his face, there were of course his boots to polish. He polished them so thoroughly, the leather reflected the morning light. It whispered, *Death!* in its shining blackness and while Vidal inhaled the smoke of his first cigarette, he imagined the sound of marching boots mixing pleasantly with the music his phonograph was spilling into the morning. The music Vidal listened to was playful and strangely different from the razor and the boots. It gave away that cruelty and death were a dance for him.

Vidal was just giving the boots the last bit of polish when Mercedes walked in with his coffee and bread.

She couldn't help but stare at the two scrawny rabbits lying on the table next to the pocket watch they'd all been warned never to touch. The kitchen maids had been gossiping all morning about what Vidal had done to the poachers who'd been looking for food to feed their family. Father and son. Mercedes took the metal coffee mug from the tray and placed it between the rabbits. So much cruelty. She'd seen too much of it in this place. Sometimes she wondered whether it covered her heart like mold by now.

"Mercedes." It always sounded like a threat when Vidal said her name, although he usually spoke to her in so soft a voice it reminded her of a cat hiding its claws under velvet fur. "Prepare those rabbits for dinner tonight."

She picked them up and inspected the skinny bodies.

"Too young to make a good meal."

Where were the sick girls they'd been supposed to feed? she wondered. Out in the yard one of the soldiers had imitated how the old man had begged for his son's life. He'd laughed while describing how Vidal had killed them both. Were they born that cruel, all these soldiers slashing and burning and killing? They had been children once like Ofelia. Mercedes feared for her. The girl was too innocent for this place and her mother wouldn't be strong enough to protect her. She was one of those women who looked for strength in men instead of finding it in her own heart.

"Well," Vidal said. "A cup of stew, then, and the meat of the hind legs."

"Yes, *señor*." Mercedes forced herself to look straight into his eyes. She didn't lower her gaze when he got up from his chair, although she feared he'd see the hatred in her eyes. If she lowered them, though, he might read that as guilt and fear, which was far more dangerous. The guilt would make him suspicious and fear would make him hungry for more.

"This coffee is burned a bit." He liked to stand close to her. "Taste it yourself."

Mercedes took the black metal mug with her left hand, still holding the two rabbits in her right. Young dead things. *You'll soon be as dead as them, Mercedes*, her heart whispered. *If you keep on doing what you're doing.*

Vidal was watching her.

48

"You should check on all these things, Mercedes. You are the house-keeper."

He put his hand, so smooth and clean, on her shoulder. Mercedes wished her dress were thicker, when he slowly moved it down her arm. The fabric was so worn, she felt his fingers on her skin.

"As you wish, *señor*."

Vidal had a great appetite for women, although they all knew he despised them. Mercedes wondered whether Ofelia's mother didn't notice the contempt in his eyes when he held her in his arms.

Vidal didn't call her back when she walked out of the room, but Mercedes felt his gaze between her shoulder blades like the tip of a knife.

She took the rabbits down to the kitchen and told Mariana, the cook, the *capitán* had complained about the coffee.

"He is nothing but a spoiled brat!" Mariana said.

The other maids laughed. Rosa, Emilia, Valeria . . . most of them had no reason to fear the *capitán*, as they rarely even saw him in person. They didn't want to see what he and his men did. Mercedes wished she could be that blind. Though maybe the older women had just seen too much to still care.

"We need one more chicken and some beef for the dinner." Mercedes filled two buckets with boiling water one of the maids had prepared. Ofelia's mother had requested a bath.

"One more chicken and some beef? Where are we supposed to find that?" Mariana mocked.

49

She was from a village close by and had two sons in the army. "Men want to fight," she liked to say. "That's how they are born." And it didn't matter to them for what they fought. What about women?

"He invited them all," Mercedes said. "The priest, the general, the doctor, the mayor and his wife too . . . and we'll have to feed them."

"And they all eat more than a stable filled with hungry pigs!" the cook called after her as Mercedes carried the buckets to the stairs.

The maids were all laughing as they brushed the rabbit blood from the table.

They didn't want to know.

8

A Princess

Ofelia didn't tell her mother about the labyrinth or the Faun. She'd felt so close to her before the Fairy came to get her. But the Faun's words echoed in her mind when she crawled back into the warm bed and Ofelia lay in the dark looking at her mother's face wondering whether she maybe wasn't her daughter.

The crescent moon. Mother.

She felt very guilty when the pale morning sun shone through the dusty windows and her mother smiled at her and kissed her forehead, as if she wished to kiss those thoughts away.

Don't betray her! Ofelia told herself while Mercedes and another maid filled the tub in the adjoining bathroom with steaming water. *She is so lonely! As lonely as I am. . . .* The tub looked as if someone had brought it from a much grander home in the city. Many such houses had been destroyed in the war that had also killed her father, and Ofelia had often played in the ruins with her friends, pretending they were the ghosts of the children who once lived in the deserted rooms.

"That bath is not for me. It's for you, Ofelia! Get up!"

Her mother smiled at her, but Ofelia knew the smile was meant for the Wolf. She wanted her daughter clean and dressed up for him, her hair combed, her shoes polished. Her mother's eyes glazed and her pale cheeks glowed when he was near, although he barely paid attention to her.

Ofelia longed to tell Mercedes about the Faun, maybe because she'd warned her about the labyrinth or because Mercedes had secrets of her own. There was a knowledge of the world in Mercedes's eyes that Ofelia didn't find in her mother's.

"Ofelia!"

Her mother looked like a bride this morning in her white dress. She sat once more in the wheelchair, as if the Wolf had stolen her feet. He had crippled her. She used to dance in the kitchen while she was cooking. Ofelia's father had always loved that. Ofelia had climbed on his lap and they'd watched her together.

"Your father is giving a dinner party tonight. Look what I made for you!"

The dress her mother held up was as green as the forest.

"Do you like it?" She caressed the silky fabric. "What I would have given to have a dress as fine as this when I was your age! I also made a white apron for it. And look at these shoes!"

They were as black and shiny as the soldiers' boots. They didn't belong in the forest and neither did the dress, although it was green.

"Do you like them?" Her mother's eyes were wide with excitement. She looked as eager to please as a scolded little girl. Ofelia felt sorry for her and embarrassed.

"Yes, Mamá," she murmured. "Yes. They are very pretty."

Her mother's eyes grew wary. *Help me*, they pleaded. *Help me to please him*. It made Ofelia feel so cold. As if she was back in the labyrinth, the shadows of its walls darkening her heart.

"Go on now." Her mother lowered her glance, her eyelids heavy with disappointment. "Take your bath before it gets cold."

All those stitches . . .

Carmen had spent so many hours sewing that dress, she didn't want to see the truth in her daughter's eyes: that she hadn't made the dress for Ofelia but for the man she told her daughter to call "Father" even though a dead man owned that title.

We all create our own fairy tales. *The dress will make him love my daughter*, that's the tale Carmen Cardoso told herself, although her heart knew Vidal only cared for the unborn child he had fathered. It is a terrible sin to betray one's child for a new love and Ofelia's mother's fingers were trembling as she opened the buttons of the dress, still smiling, pretending life and love were what she wanted them to be.

The bathroom was filled with white veils of steam. Ofelia felt it warm and wet on her skin when she closed the door behind her. The tub looked like an inviting white porcelain boat ready to leave for the moon, but the hot bath was not the reason why Ofelia was eager to finally be alone.

She'd hidden the Faun's book and the little pouch behind the bathroom radiator last night, afraid her mother would find them. It was her secret, and apart from her mother's dislike for books, she was worried the Faun's gift might lose its magic if anyone else saw or touched it.

She could barely hold the heavy book on her lap when she sat down on the edge of the bathtub. Its leather binding felt like weathered tree bark and the pages were still empty, but she somehow knew that would change. All the truly important things hide from view. Ofelia was still young enough to know that.

And indeed, one of the blank pages began to bleed brown and pale green ink the moment Ofelia touched it. An illustration of a toad emerged on the page on the right, then of a hand and of a labyrinth. Flowers began to cover the edge of the page and at its center the image of a tree took shape, old and crooked, its leafless branches bent like horns, its trunk split and hollow.

A girl was kneeling inside and peering out at Ofelia. Her feet were bare but she was wearing a green dress and a white apron just like those Ofelia's mother had made. Once the image on the right-hand page was finished, the left-hand page began to fill with sepia brown letters, as old-fashioned as if an invisible illuminator were writing them with a brush bound from the hairs of a marten's tail. The letters were so beautiful for a few moments Ofelia just admired them, but then she began to read:

> *Once upon a time, when the woods were young,*
>
> *they were home to creatures*
>
> *who were full of magic and wonder. . . .*

"Ofelia!" Her mother knocked at the door. "Hurry up! I want to see the dress on you. I want you to be beautiful. For the *capitán*."

Betrayal . . .

Ofelia stepped in front of the mirror. Steam covered the glass, blurring her reflection. Ofelia pushed her bathrobe from her left shoulder.

"You will look like a princess!" her mother called through the door.

Ofelia stared at her reflection.

There it was: a sickle moon surrounded by three stars, as clearly as if someone had drawn them onto her skin with the sepia ink that had filled the pages of the book. The Faun had told the truth.

"A princess," Ofelia whispered.

She looked at her reflection.

And she smiled.

9

MILK AND MEDICINE

Of course, there would be enough food for the *capitán*'s dinner guests. His soldiers made sure of that and everyone in the kitchen knew how. Some local families would go hungry for a few days, but what was there to say when soldiers knocked on the door to claim the last chicken or the potatoes a farmer had hidden for his children? Mercedes felt so ashamed as she and the other maids chopped vegetables. That was the use of knives for women: to cut food for the men who killed with their knives . . . who killed those women's husbands, their sons, and their daughters.

The knife she sliced onions with was the same most kitchen maids kept in the folds of their aprons, right below the belly, safe and always handy: it

56

had a short blade, roughly three inches in length, made of cheap steel and a worn wooden handle.

Mercedes couldn't take her eyes off the blade. She still remembered the *capitán*'s hand on her arm. What if he wouldn't let her go one day? The others for sure didn't guess her thoughts when she folded her stained apron around the slim blade. They were laughing and gossiping to make themselves forget the uniforms outside and that their sons were fighting each other. And maybe they were right. Maybe life was still more than that. There was still the silence of the forest and the warmth of the sun, the light of the moon. Mercedes yearned to join in the laughter, but her heart was so tired. It had been afraid for too long.

"Make sure those chickens are cleaned properly," she said. "And don't forget the beans."

Her voice sounded harsher than she had intended, but the others weren't paying attention to her anyway. They were all smiling looking at Ofelia, who was standing in the kitchen doorway wearing the green dress and the white apron Mercedes had ironed with the same care Ofelia's mother had put into making them. The clothes made the girl look like a character from a book Mercedes had loved as a child. Her mother had often brought books home for her and her brother. She'd been a teacher, but all her books couldn't protect her when soldiers burned their village. The flames had eaten both her mother and her books.

"You look wonderful, girl!" the cook exclaimed. "Just beautiful."

"Yes! That's such a beautiful dress!" Rosa said, her face soft with tenderness. She had a daughter Ofelia's age. The girl reminded them all of their children and grandchildren—and of the girls they had once been themselves.

"Get back to work! Stop wasting time," Mercedes told them off, although she felt the tenderness in her heart too.

She walked over to Ofelia and gently straightened the collar of her dress. Her mother was really a talented seamstress and for a moment the dress she'd made for her daughter cast a spell in the old mill's kitchen—the dress and the girl's beaming face, so bright with happiness and beauty like a freshly opened flower. Yes, for a moment it made them all believe the world to be peaceful and whole again.

"Do you want some milk with honey?"

Ofelia nodded and Mercedes took her outside where the brown cow was standing under the trees, her udder firm with milk. It ran warm and white over Mercedes's fingers as she filled a bucket with it.

"Move back," she softly said to Ofelia. "We can't have you getting milk on your dress. It makes you look like a princess."

Ofelia hesitantly took a step back.

"Do you believe in Fairies, Mercedes?" she asked as she caressed the cow's smooth flank.

Mercedes squeezed the cow's teats once more. "No. But when I was a little girl I did. I believed in a lot of things I don't believe anymore."

The cow mooed impatiently. She wanted to feed calves, not men. Mercedes calmed her with her hands and a few soft words.

Ofelia forgot about the dress and the milk and stepped to her side.

"Last night a Fairy visited me," she said softly.

"Really?" Mercedes dipped a small bowl into the bucket and filled it with the warm milk.

Ofelia nodded, wide-eyed. "Yes. And she wasn't alone! There were three of them. And a Faun, too!"

"A Faun?" Mercedes straightened up.

"Yes. He was so old . . . . and very tall and thin." Ofelia traced a huge figure in the air with her hands. "He looked old and smelled old . . . musty. Like earth when it's wet with rain. And a little bit like this cow."

And I want you to know, she seemed to say with her eyes. *Please believe me, Mercedes!* It is hard to have secrets one cannot share, or to believe in a truth that others don't want to see. Mercedes knew all about it.

"A Faun," she repeated. "My mother warned me to be wary of Fauns. Sometimes they are good, sometimes they're not. . . ."

The memory brought a smile to her lips—the memory and the girl. But it faded when she saw the *capitán* walking toward her with one of his officers by his side. The world immediately filled with shadows.

"Mercedes!"

He ignored the girl so completely that for a moment he made Mercedes almost believe Ofelia wasn't there.

"Follow me. I need you at the barn."

She went with him. Of course. Although she would have loved to stay with the girl and the warm milk and the breath of the cow on her skin.

59

A few soldiers were unloading a truck in front of the barn.

Lieutenant Medem, the officer in command, saluted Vidal.

"We brought everything, Capitán. As promised." The lieutenant's uniform was as stiff and clean as a toy soldier's. "Flour, salt, oil, medicine," he listed, while leading the way into the barn. "Olives, bacon . . ." He pointed proudly at the baskets and cartons. The dusty shelves were filled with packages and cans.

Vidal sniffed at a small package wrapped in brown paper. He liked his tobacco. And his liquor.

"And here are the ration cards." The few dozen vouchers Lieutenant Medem handed Vidal were precious property at a time when the war had burned harvests and even the farmers couldn't feed their children, because the army controlled what was left. The boxes Medem's men had brought to the mill could have fed more than one village. But Mercedes didn't look at the boxes that contained food. She had stopped at a stack whose labels depicted a red cross. Medicine. More than enough to heal almost every wound. Including a leg wound.

"Mercedes." Vidal was inspecting the lock on the barn door. "The key."

She took a key from the key ring in her pocket and handed it to him.

"Is this the only one?"

She nodded.

"From now on I'll carry it."

There was that glance again. What did he know?

"Capitán!" Garces, the officer who called from outside, was as lean as a weasel and always had a smile for the maids.

Vidal ignored him. He continued to look at Mercedes, the key in his hand, his gaze both threatening and teasing, playing his favorite game: the game of fear.

He knows, she thought once again. *No, he doesn't, Mercedes. It's the way he looks at everyone.* She exhaled deeply when he finally turned and stepped outside. *Breathe, Mercedes.*

Vidal joined Garces, who was scrutinizing the forest through his binoculars.

"Maybe it's nothing, Capitán," Mercedes heard him say as he handed the binoculars to Vidal, but she could see it with her bare eyes: a fine, almost invisible trace of smoke was rising from the canopy of the trees, drawing a treacherous line into the blue sky.

Vidal lowered the binoculars. "No. It's them. I am sure."

They were astride their horses within moments. Mercedes watched them ride off into the forest. Only men lit fires, men the soldiers had come to hunt.

Breathe, Mercedes.

THE LABYRINTH

Once upon a time, there was a nobleman named Francisco Ayuso who liked to hunt in the forest near his palace. It was an old forest, very old, and he felt so young among its trees.

One day Ayuso and his men were following a rare stag with fur as silvery as the light of the moon. His men lost the stag's track near an old mill, and when Ayuso dismounted his horse to refresh himself at the mill's pond, he found a young woman asleep on the ground between the watercress and dragon lilies. Her hair was as black as a raven's feathers, her skin as pale as the petals of the whitest rose in Ayuso's palace gardens.

She woke with a start when he touched her shoulder and backed away from him, hiding behind a tree, like a deer chased by his hounds. It took Ayuso a while to convince her of his good intentions. She looked like she hadn't eaten for days so he told his men to bring her food. When asked for her name, she told them she couldn't remember it, so one of his soldiers suspected she might be a surviving victim of the Pale Man, a creature who roamed the area stealing children from the surrounding villages and dragging them to his underground lair.

Only two victims were known to have escaped the Pale Man, bringing back terrible tales of children being eaten alive and a monster so horrible that they didn't dare fall asleep for fear they'd meet him again in their dreams. However, when Ayuso asked the young woman about the Pale Man, she just shook her head and the expression on her face was so lost, he spared her any further questions, worried they would stir memories she'd been wise enough to forget.

She clearly had no home, so Ayuso invited her to his palace. He gave her a room and new clothes and called her Alba, as her memory was as blank as a white sheet. She soon walked in his gardens and enjoyed his roses, and after just a few days they both wished for nothing but each other's company.

After three months Francisco Ayuso asked Alba to be his wife, and she accepted, as she loved him as much as Francisco loved her. A year later she gave birth to a son. Alba loved the boy as tenderly as she loved her husband, but each time she looked at the child she felt a great sadness because she couldn't tell him who she was or where she came from. She became restless and started to spend hours wandering through the forest or sitting by the pond of the old mill.

Not far from the mill lived a woman called Rocio, who had a reputation for being a witch. She lived with her daughter and son in a hut near the Split Tree, which was said to house a poisonous toad between its roots. People whispered that Rocio's potions could grant true love, a long life, or, if desired, the death of an enemy, but most women who came to see her asked for help with an unwanted pregnancy, as they could barely feed their living children.

One afternoon, the soldier Ayuso had secretly ordered to follow Alba to make sure she was safe in the forest came back with the news that Alba had been visiting Rocio. Ayuso was very upset and confronted Alba, who begged him to understand she'd only asked Rocio to help her find out who she was. Rocio had told her the answer to her question would only be revealed on a full moon night in a labyrinth that must be built behind the millpond from the stones of a nearby village, which had been deserted ever since three children had been taken by the Pale Man.

Ayuso loved Alba more than anything else in the world, so he had Rocio the witch brought to him to learn exactly how to build the labyrinth. Rocio took him to the place where she'd envisioned it. She marked the four corners with stones and drew the patterns of the walls with a willow branch onto the forest soil. At the center, she told Ayuso, he'd have to build a well and, inside, a staircase leading down to its bottom. Ayuso didn't like the way she looked at him. It felt as if she could see his darkest desires—as clearly as if his heart were made from glass. She frightened him, and he despised her for that.

"I will do as you say," he said, "but if you make a fool of me, and my wife does not find what she has lost, I will have you drowned in the millpond."

Rocio answered him with a smile.

"I know," she said. "But we all have to play our parts, don't we?"

Then she walked back to her hut.

It took two months to build the labyrinth. Ayuso's workers used only stones from the deserted village, as the witch had directed, and built the walls, the well, and the stairs exactly as the witch had described them.

Alba had to wait seven nights until the moon rose like a silver coin above the finished labyrinth, casting the shadow of the arch the workers had crafted to span the entrance onto the mossy forest floor. They adorned the arch with the horned head of Cernunnos, a pagan god who had once been worshipped in these woods. Rocio, it was said, still prayed to him.

From dusk till dawn that night Alba stayed in the labyrinth, walking its crooked paths, even though her infant son was crying for her milk in her chambers. Ayuso didn't follow her, afraid the labyrinth wouldn't reveal the answers his wife so desperately yearned for in his presence. He waited all night in front of the labyrinth and when Alba finally came out, Ayuso saw in her face that she hadn't found what she'd been looking for.

Every month for the next twelve months, on the night of the full moon, Alba went back into the labyrinth, but all she found between its stone walls was silence, and her sadness grew and grew until one moonless November night, she fell gravely ill. She died before the moon was full again, and one hour after she drew her last breath, Ayuso sent five of his soldiers to the witch's hut. They dragged Rocio through the woods and into the millpond, although the miller begged them not to curse his mill with such a deed. It took three men to drown her. They left her body drifting between the lily pads for the fish to eat.

Fifteen years later, Ayuso's son walked into the labyrinth hoping to find his mother there. He was never seen again, and it took another two hundred and twenty-three years until the prophecy of the witch came true and the labyrinth revealed his mother's true name when she once again walked its ancient corridors as a girl called Ofelia.

10

THE TREE

Ofelia had already walked deep into the forest when she heard the horses behind her. But they didn't head in her direction and soon the murmuring of the trees was louder than the fading hoofbeats. Ofelia read the words from the Faun's book while she walked. They sounded even more enchanting under the trees—and she read them over and over, although it was not easy to walk holding the open book:

Once upon a time, when the woods were young,
they were home to creatures
who were full of magic and wonder.

Ofelia's feet followed the rhythm of the words as if they were drawing an invisible path.

The creatures protected one another.
They slept in the shade of a colossal fig tree
that grew on a hill near the mill.

Ofelia looked up from the book and there was the hill. It wasn't terribly steep, she could climb it with just a few steps, but it would have taken five men to embrace the tree growing on it. The trunk was split, exactly as the book had shown her.

But now the tree is dying.
Its branches are dry,
its trunk old and twisted.

She looked up at the two huge leafless branches growing from the trunk, bent like the horns of the Faun.

There were still more words in the book. Ofelia whispered them as her eyes followed the pale brown ink across the pages.

A monstrous toad has settled in its roots
and won't let the tree thrive.
You must put the three magic stones
into the Toad's mouth.

69

Ofelia opened the pouch the Faun had given her. Three small stones fell into her hand. And the book still held two more lines:

Retrieve the golden key from inside his belly.
Only then will the fig tree flourish again.

From inside his belly . . . Ofelia closed the book and looked at the gaping cleft in the tree. It was very dark inside. She slipped the three stones back into the pouch and took a step toward the tree, when she realized with a start that her new shoes were covered in mud. The heroes in her fairy-tale books never worried about their shoes or their clothes, but Ofelia took off the white apron and her new green dress and hung them over a branch. She could imagine all too well how upset her mother would be if she ruined them. Then she slipped off her shoes and approached the tree. The ground was cold under her bare feet and the wind made her shudder in her thin underdress. The cleft was high enough for her to step through, but the tunnel beyond it was so narrow that Ofelia had to get down on her hands and knees.

Outside the wind was tearing at the ribbons of her new dress.

Beware, it whispered.

Beware, Ofelia, the fluttering ribbons sang.

But Ofelia was already crawling down the tunnel—into the wet wooden intestines of the dying tree. Soon slimy mud covered her hands and knees. It soaked her white underdress and dyed it the colors of the earth. The tree's roots were all around her, weaving through the wet soil and reaching into the ground like the claws of a huge wooden creature. Woodlice as big as mice crawled up Ofelia's arms and the mud squelched under her hands as if the ground yearned to devour her.

There seemed to be no end to the tunnel and the maze of roots, but Ofelia wouldn't turn back. She had to fulfill the Faun's tasks before the moon was full if she wanted to prove to herself and to him he was right: that she was Moanna, the princess whose father was waiting for her even though Death had made her believe she lost him. For if she was not Moanna, who else would she be? The daughter of a wolf who had stolen her mother's heart and spelled *murder* with his eyes. Ofelia stopped for a moment to listen to the sounds of the earth and her own fiercely beating heart. Then she once again sank her hands into the mud and continued to crawl down the endless tunnel.

11

THE CREATURES OF THE FOREST

It didn't take Vidal and his soldiers long to find the remains of the campfire that had sent the treacherous smoke into the sky. Branches were still smoldering when he got off his horse and knelt beside it, and he could still feel the heat when he took off his glove to hold his bare hand over the embers.

Yes. They'd been here less than twenty minutes ago.

The rebels must have heard them coming. Of course. Vidal stared at the trees, wishing he could hunt as silently as a wolf. He would have torn them apart by now and licked their blood off the moss that was covered with ash from their fire.

Garces knelt by his *capitán*'s side. Vidal liked the devotion in his eyes.

72

Garces listened to every word from his lips as devoutly as an altar server read the words from a priest's lips at Mass.

"A dozen men. Not more." Vidal had learned to track from his grandfather. His father had only taught him that the worst beasts walk on two legs.

"What do we have here?" He brushed a few wilted leaves aside. A small package was lying between the stones that surrounded the fireplace. They had indeed left in haste. The three glass vials, carefully wrapped in brown paper, looked familiar. Vidal rose to his feet. He held one of the vials up and let the clear liquid catch the sunlight. Antibiotics. That probably meant that at least one of the rebels was wounded. Good.

"*Mierda*, look at this!" Garces grabbed a small piece of paper from the ground. "They lost a lottery ticket!"

He laughed.

Vidal silenced him with a gesture. He took a step and listened. They were still here. He could sense it. Those rebel sons of bitches were watching them! He took another step, but all he could hear were the sounds of the forest. Curse it!

"Hey!" he yelled into the trees, holding up the vial. "You left this behind! And what about your lottery ticket? Why don't you come back and get it? Who knows? This could be your lucky day."

The only reply was the chirp of a bird.

And the rustling of leaves in the wind.

The forest was mocking him.

Again.

No. Vidal turned around. He wouldn't make a fool of himself by chasing the bastards through this treacherous maze of trees. He would wait for them to come to him, for he had the food and the medicine. The vials were proof they needed it.

Vidal was right.

His prey was watching. The soldiers mounted their horses and followed their *capitán* back to the mill, the trees painting their uniforms black with their shadows. And a dozen men in ragged clothes who were hiding on a hill above the abandoned campfire were watching their hunters ride away. For now.

Vidal had almost found them this time.

He would find them again.

12

THE TOAD

Ofelia had given up wiping the woodlice from her arms and face, which by now were covered solidly in mud. She felt as if she would be crawling through the intestines of the earth forever. The lost princess, if the Faun was right, looking for her underground kingdom.

She found it harder and harder to breathe, and all the tunnel had revealed so far was darkness. Darkness, roots, wet soil, and armies of woodlice serving whom? Ofelia had just asked herself that question when she heard something moving behind her, something heavy and huge.

She peered over her mud-covered shoulder to see a massive toad just a few feet behind her. His wart-covered body was as large as a cow and he

75

was plugging the whole tunnel. The Faun's book had portrayed the creature quite perfectly, but he'd looked so much smaller in the illustration!

"H-hello," Ofelia stuttered. "I am Princess Moanna, and I . . ." She took a deep breath. "I am not afraid of you."

That was of course not the truth, but hopefully the Toad couldn't read a human face. Ofelia could for sure not read his. A belching croak escaped the bloated body, while the golden eyes were blinking as if the huge beast couldn't believe something so furless and fragile had crawled all the way down to his lair.

Ofelia kept her eyes on the creature as she opened the pouch and let the three stones slip into her palm. All around her the mud was alive with woodlice.

"Aren't you ashamed?" she asked, her voice shaking even more than her sore knees. "To live down here eating all these bugs, growing fat, while the tree is dying?" She swatted a woodlouse from her arm while another crawled over her cheek.

The Toad's answer was swift. He unfurled his enormous sticky tongue and slapped it across Ofelia's face. It grasped the woodlouse and left her cheek dripping with saliva. But what was worse—her fingers let go of the Faun's stones!

The Toad drew his tongue back into his gaping mouth, while Ofelia desperately searched for the stones in the mud.

The Toad was quite annoyed with the furless creature.

He was sure the Tree had sent her. Groaning angrily, he opened his mouth and showered the intruder with the poisonous slime that was eating the Tree's wooden heart. Oh yes. It would for sure eat the furless flesh of his uninvited visitor as well. The Toad was vastly satisfied with himself.

Ofelia wasn't giving up, despite the venomous slime burning her face and arms. She opened her trembling hand and saw that along with the stones she'd plucked from the mud, she'd grabbed a few woodlice that were rolling and unrolling themselves on her palm. Rolled up they looked exactly like the stones.

"Hey!" she called, holding up the scrambling insects. She could only hope she'd grabbed the right stones along with the woodlice. The mud made them all look alike.

The Toad licked his lips, while he stared at her outstretched hand with his golden eyes.

Finally!

The intruder showed at least some respect. He was very pleased, although her offerings were poor. The Toad loved to devour his servants. He found the crunching sound they made when he cracked them with his toothless gums to be very satisfying.

Yes, he would accept the offering.

Ofelia didn't move when the huge tongue slashed through the air like a whip. It enveloped her hand so firmly she was sure the Toad would rip it off. But she still had her hand when the tongue withdrew, and—Ofelia looked at her fingers dripping with saliva—both the woodlice and the stones were gone.

It took the Toad a moment to swallow and digest his prey. So long a moment that Ofelia was already sure she'd grabbed the wrong stones or that the Faun's gift had failed.

But then the Toad opened his mouth.

He opened it wider and wider.

Oh, how his intestines were burning!

As if they'd just been filled with his own poison!

And his skin . . . it was crawling, as if all his woodlice servants had begun to eat him alive! Oh, he should have strangled that pale-skinned creature with his tongue! Only now did he realize what she had come for. He saw it in her treacherous eyes. His golden treasure! But that realization came too late. With his last dying breath he retched out his own stomach, a mass of pulsating amber flesh, and his huge body deflated like a torn balloon leaving behind nothing but a lifeless pile of skin.

Ofelia crawled to the lump of flesh, though the sight and smell of it made her sick. And there it was! The key the Faun had asked her to bring was sticking to the Toad's entrails along with dozens of twitching woodlice. The slime covering it stretched like the shimmering threads of a spider when Ofelia grabbed it, but finally it let go.

The key was longer than Ofelia's hand and very beautiful. She clenched it all the way back through the endless tunnel, although it wasn't easy to crawl with just one hand. When she finally stumbled out of the broken tree, the sky was already dark and rain was pouring through the canopy of the leaves. How long had she been gone? All the joy she had felt about completing her task and getting the key vanished. The dinner! Her new dress!

Ofelia stumbled to the branch where she'd hung her clothes.

But the dress was gone and so was the apron.

The fear piercing her heart was almost as grim as the fear she had felt in the Toad's tunnels. She sobbed as she searched the forest floor, pressing the key to her chest, which was so cold from all the mud and the rain. When she finally found the dress just a little way from the tree, the green fabric was caked in mud, and the white apron was so dirty it was nearly invisible in the dark. Above her the branches creaked in the wind and Ofelia thought she heard her mother's heart break.

The rain was so strong by now that it washed most of the mud off Ofelia's face and limbs. It was as if the night was trying to comfort her. In her despair Ofelia held up the dress and the apron into the falling rain, but even a million of its cold drops couldn't turn them green and white again.

THE TAILOR'S WIFE

Vidal hated the rain almost as much as he hated the forest. It touched his body, his hair, and his clothes and made him feel vulnerable. Human.

He had lined up his soldiers nearly an hour ago, but his guests were all late and his men looked like dripping scarecrows. Yes. Vidal stared at his watch. They were late. Its broken face told him that and other things—that he was in the wrong place, that his father's shadow still made him as invisible as the men he was hunting, that the rain and the forest would beat him.

No. He stared over the yard, where the waxing moon was reflecting in the puddles. No, although the rain stained his immaculate uniform and covered his polished boots with mud, he wouldn't let this place beat him. It felt like an answer from a grim god who liked men as lost and twisted as

Vidal, when the headlights of two cars pierced the night. His men rushed forward to shield the passengers with umbrellas. They had all come, everyone who considered himself important in this wretched place: the general and one of his commanding officers; the mayor and his wife; a rich widow, who had been a member of the Fascist party since 1935; the priest; and Dr. Ferreira. Yes, Vidal had invited the good doctor too. Not without reason. He offered his umbrella to the mayor's wife and led her into the house.

Mercedes had brought Ofelia's mother down in her wheelchair. Carmen reminded Mercedes of a girl who'd been taught to not offend her father and now did the same for her husband, making herself small, even when she wasn't in the wheelchair.

"Have you checked for her in the garden?" Carmen muttered as Mercedes pushed her into the room, which the maids had transformed once again from a war room into a dining room.

"Yes, Señora."

Mercedes had checked everywhere for Ofelia, in the barn, in the stables, even at the old labyrinth. She saw fear in the other woman's eyes, but not for her child, no. She was afraid to upset her new husband. Everyone at the mill was sure Vidal had only married her for the unborn child. Mercedes saw the same belief on the faces of his guests.

"May I introduce you all to my wife, Carmen?"

Vidal couldn't hide that he was ashamed of her. The women among his guests were far better dressed, and their jewelry made the earrings that Ofelia's mother wore resemble a child's cheap play jewelry. The mayor's wife hid her contempt behind a bright smile, but the widow didn't make that effort.

81

Look at her, her face said. *Where did he find her? She's a little Cinderella, isn't she?*

Dr. Ferreira exchanged a glance with Mercedes before he sat down at the table. He was afraid, she could read it in his face. Afraid that he'd been invited to this dinner, because Vidal knew and Mercedes prayed that his fear wouldn't give them both away. She didn't know to whom she prayed now, to the forest, to the night, to the moon . . . ? It was for sure not the god the men who were taking their seats at the table prayed to. He had deserted her too often.

"Only one?" The priest took a voucher from the stack Vidal handed to him and passed the others on.

"I am not sure that is enough, Capitán," the mayor said. "We meet a lot of dissatisfaction caused by the continuous shortages of even the most basic foods."

"If people are careful," the priest said, hastily coming to Vidal's aid, "one voucher should be plenty."

The priest liked to please the military. The other maids who still went to church every Sunday had told Mercedes how he sang the praises of obedience and order from the pulpit and condemned the men in the woods as pagans and communists in his sermons, no better than the devil.

"We have of course plenty of food now," Vidal said, "but we have to make sure no one gets enough to feed the rebels. They're losing ground and one of them is wounded."

Dr. Ferreira hid the slight tremble of his lips by wiping his mouth with his napkin. "Wounded?" he asked in a casual voice. "How can you be so sure, Capitán?"

"Because we almost got them today. And we found this." Vidal held up one of the vials they had found in the forest.

Mercedes caught another glance from Ferreira. She straightened her back and tried her best to give him confidence by banning any expression of worry from her face, though she tasted her own fear like vinegar in her mouth.

"May God save their lost souls. What happens to their bodies hardly matters to Him." The priest sank his fork into a roasted potato.

"We'll help you in any way we can, Capitán," the mayor said. "We know you're not here by choice."

Vidal straightened up in his chair. It was his usual gesture when something offended him. Getting ready for attack.

"But you're wrong, sir," he said with a stiff smile. "I choose to be here because I want my son to be born in a new, clean Spain. Our enemies"—he paused to look at his guests, one after the other—"hold the mistaken belief that we're all created equal. But there's a big difference: They lost this war. We won. And if we need to kill each and every one of them to make that clear, then that's what we'll do. Each and every one of them." He raised his wineglass. "To choice!"

His guests raised their glasses. Dr. Ferreira joined them, clenching his glass firmly.

"To choice!" the voices echoed through the room. Mercedes was glad she didn't hear them anymore when she slipped out of the door and returned to the kitchen.

"Put the coffee on," she ordered the other maids. "I'll get some more firewood," she added, grabbing her jacket from the hook by the kitchen door.

They all watched her silently when she lit a lantern—the match in her hand visibly shaking—and stepped out into the rain.

She walked past the cars and the soldiers guarding them, with her head down, hoping to be invisible to them as usual, just a maid. But it was so hard to not hasten her steps. *Because we almost got them today.*

Mercedes stopped when she reached the edge of the forest. She cast one more glance over her shoulder, making sure branches were shielding her from the guards' view, then she raised the lantern and moved her hand up and down over the light—once, twice, three times. So far, this signal had always worked. Her brother usually had a man watching the mill in case she had a message or news for them. Only when Mercedes lowered the lantern and turned to walk back to the house did she notice a small figure between the trees. So small and trembling in her wet clothes.

"Ofelia?"

The girl's body was as cold as ice and her dark eyes were wide with worry. But there was something else in them: a pride and strength her mother lacked. Ofelia was clutching something in her hand, but Mercedes didn't ask what it was or where the girl had been. Who knew better than her about secrets that are best kept inside? She put her arm around Ofelia's shivering shoulders and led her back to the mill, hoping the girl's secrets were not as dangerous as her own.

❦

"So how did you two meet?" The mayor's wife smiled and Ofelia's mother forgot the contempt on the other guests' faces. She should have known better.

It's so much safer to stay silent and invisible when you feel weak and small. But this was her fairy tale and Carmen wished so hard for it to end well.

"Ofelia's father used to make the *capitán*'s uniforms."

"Oh, I see!"

Carmen didn't realize that was all the mayor's wife needed to know. A tailor's wife . . . a previously married woman. The faces around the table stiffened. But Ofelia's mother was still lost in her fairy tale. *Once upon a time . . .*

She rested her hand tenderly on Vidal's. "After my husband died, I went to work at the shop, on my own . . ."

The other women looked down at their plates. What a confession! In their world a woman only worked if she was poor and had to support a family. But Ofelia's mother still believed the prince had saved her from all that: the poverty, the shame, the helplessness . . . She looked at Vidal, her eyes bright with love.

"And then, a little more than a year ago"—she still had her hand on his—"we met again."

"How curious." The pearls the mayor's wife wore around her neck shimmered as if she'd stolen a few stars from the sky. "Finding each other again like that . . ."

There was a hint of warmth in her voice. The tailor's wife and the soldier . . . everyone loves a fairy tale.

"Curious. Oh yes, yes, very curious," the rich widow said, curling her lips. She only believed in fairy tales where a hero brings home heaps of gold.

"Please forgive my wife." Vidal freed his hand and picked up his glass. "She thinks these silly stories are interesting to others."

Carmen Cardoso stared down at her plate in embarrassment. There were fairy tales describing dinners like this. Maybe her daughter should have warned her that she had mistaken a Bluebeard for a prince?

Mercedes saw Carmen's sunken shoulders as she walked back into the room, and she was glad it was good news she whispered into Carmen's ear.

"Please excuse me," Carmen Cardoso murmured. "My daughter, she is . . ." She didn't finish the sentence.

Nobody looked at her when Mercedes pulled her wheelchair from the table.

"Did I tell you that I knew your father, Capitán?" the general asked as Mercedes pushed the wheelchair toward the door. "We both fought in Morocco. I knew him only briefly, but he left a great impression."

"Really? I had no idea."

Mercedes could hear in Vidal's voice that he didn't like the question.

"His soldiers said," the general continued, "that when General Vidal died on the battlefield, he smashed his silver pocket watch on a rock to make sure his son would know the exact hour and minute of his death. And to show him how a brave man dies."

"Nonsense!" Vidal said. "My father never owned a pocket watch."

Mercedes longed to pull the pocket watch out of his jacket to show them all what a broken, lying thing he was. But instead she pushed the wheelchair out of the room. The girl was waiting. Mercedes had left Ofelia upstairs taking a hot bath to drive the cold away and she'd tried to wash the dress, but it was ruined.

86

Ofelia evaded her mother's eyes when Mercedes pushed the wheelchair into the bathroom. There was still that hint of pride on the girl's face and a rebelliousness Mercedes hadn't noticed before. She liked it much better than the sadness, which had followed Ofelia like a shadow when she arrived at the mill. Her mother didn't feel that way. She picked the ruined dress up from the tile floor and ran her hand over the stained fabrics.

"What you've done hurts me, Ofelia."

Mercedes left them alone and Ofelia let herself sink deeper into the hot water. She could still feel the woodlice crawling on her arms and legs, but she had fulfilled the Faun's first task. Nothing else mattered, not even her mother's upset face.

"When you've finished your bath, you'll go to bed without supper, Ofelia," she heard her say. "Are you listening? Sometimes I think you'll never learn to behave."

Ofelia still didn't look at her. The foam on the water showed her reflection in a thousand shimmering bubbles. Princess Moanna.

"You're disappointing me, Ofelia. And your father, too."

The wheelchair didn't turn easily on the tiles. When Ofelia lifted her head, her mother was already at the door.

Her father . . . Ofelia smiled. Her father was a tailor. And a king.

She heard the soft flutter of wings the moment her mother closed the bathroom door behind her. The Fairy landed on the bathtub edge. She was wearing her insect body again.

"I've got the key!" Ofelia whispered. "Take me to the labyrinth!"

The Mill That Lost Its Pond

Once upon a time, when magic did not hide from human eyes as thoroughly as it does today, there was a mill in the middle of a forest, which was said to be cursed by the death of a witch who'd been drowned by a nobleman's soldiers in its pond.

The flour the mill produced turned black every year on the anniversary of the witch's death and as not even the cats keeping the mice away from the farmers' corn would go near it, Javier the miller would throw the ruined flour into the woods. The flour was always gone the next morning, as if the trees had devoured it with their roots.

This went on for seven years. The witch had died on a foggy November day and when the eighth anniversary of her death dawned, the ground behind the mill was white with freshly fallen snow. The flour the miller threw onto the frozen forest floor seemed even blacker than it had the year before, so black it looked as if the night itself had fallen from the sky to make room for the day.

As always on the following morning the flour was gone, but this time a few remnants blackened a trail of footprints. The miller followed the footprints all the way to the millpond. The thin layer of ice covering the surface was broken, black flour drifting on the water like ash.

The miller's heart filled with fear as cold as the broken ice and he nearly stumbled over his own feet as he backed away from the pond. He had witnessed the drowning of Rocio eight years ago. He had tried to pull her lifeless body to the shore after the nobleman's soldiers had left, but the vines that grew as densely in the pond as a waterman's green hair had kept the woman's body firmly in their grip. When the miller had finally rowed his boat out to get her, the body had already sunk to the bottom of the pond. *What if she is still there?* he asked himself. What if Rocio was coming to take revenge on him because he hadn't saved her from her murderers even though he'd known her since childhood and she'd once healed his wife of a terrible fever?

The miller stepped closer to the water to at least get a glimpse of the creature whose footprints, blackened by the cursed flour, looked so human. *Be careful, Javier!* the trees whispered with their barren branches. *What's in there was bred by murder and cruelty. The sins of men are not forgotten. They bring forth poisonous fruit.*

But men don't hear what the trees say. They have forgotten how to listen to the wild things, and the miller took another step toward the pond. Something moved under the ice. It was as silvery as the moon Rocio used to dance beneath.

The face emerging from the water appeared female, and was so beautiful the miller took another step forward. The eyes of the creature resembled the golden eyes of a toad and the hands reaching out for him had webs between each finger. The miller didn't care. He yearned for the touch of those hands more than he'd ever yearned for his wife's embrace, more than he'd ever yearned for anything. He waded into the water and embraced the shimmering body even though it felt like ice in his arms. The creature's lips were covered with black flour and the miller felt his heart become as silvery and cold as hers when he kissed them, but he couldn't let go and they both sank into the pond, united in a fierce embrace.

When her husband did not return late in the day, the miller's wife went looking for him. She followed two sets of footsteps, one of them her husband's, into the woods and to the pond, where she called his name over the dark water. When there was no response she ran to the village where her parents lived and yelled across the marketplace that the witch in the pond had devoured her husband.

Soon an angry crowd headed for the pond with nets, pitchforks, and clubs. They stopped at the shore where the miller's tracks disappeared into the water. Something was shimmering in the depths of the pond like sunken silver treasure, and the villagers forgot about the tears of the miller's wife. All they could think of was the silver and, when their nets couldn't bring it up, they set fire to their clubs and to every branch they could find on the frozen ground, setting them adrift on the pond until it was covered with flames and the water turned into white smoke.

The villagers kept the fire going until they'd chopped and burned all the surrounding trees, and all that was left of the pond were dead fish and pebbles covered in soot. The lump of silver lying among them resembled two lovers melted into one.

The villagers backed away and the miller's wife screamed and fell on her knees as she recognized her husband's features in one of the faces melted together in a kiss. No one dared touch the silver, and the wife went back to the village with the others never to return.

From then on the mill stood deserted, as what use is a mill without a pond? Then, after almost ninety years, a man moved in, who, as rumors said, had once been a famous watchmaker in the great and faraway city of Madrid. His dogs chased every man, woman, and child who came near the mill. Some even claimed he was guarded by a pack of man-eating wolves. A rabbit poacher once managed to peek through the windows without being torn to pieces and, while selling his poached rabbits to a butcher, reported that the mill's new owner had brought the silver up from the dead pond and was melting it down to make watches.

14

KEEP THE KEY

The heart of the labyrinth still looked the same, a long-forgotten place at the bottom of the world. But Ofelia felt more hesitant to climb down the stairs to the column this time. It is often easier to find something out than to face what you've found.

The walls along the steps were covered with niches. Ofelia hadn't noticed them during her first visit. They looked like votive sites awaiting offerings for a forgotten god, or the bricked-in windows of a sunken tower. Everything in the labyrinth spoke of forgotten things . . . though maybe they weren't forgotten. Maybe they were being kept safe.

The Fairy was clearly thrilled to be back. She swirled and fluttered

93

around like someone happy to be home. While they were waiting for the Faun Ofelia took a closer look at the column. A girl holding a baby was carved into the stone. She had no face, time had wiped it away, but the figure standing behind her, his clawed hand on the girl's shoulder, was clearly the Faun, protecting her, holding her—or holding her down.

Ofelia was just touching the weathered face of the baby when the Faun appeared from the shadows. He looked different. Younger. Stronger. More dangerous.

"I got the key," Ofelia said proudly, holding it up.

But the Faun just nodded. Ofelia had expected a bit more than that. After all she'd faced a giant toad and saved the fig tree, not to speak of offending her mother. The Faun, though, seemed far more excited about what he was eating. Ofelia couldn't quite make out what it was, only that it was bloody and raw, maybe a dead bird or a rodent.

The Faun ripped off a mouthful with his sharp, pointed teeth and took a few prancing steps toward her.

"That's me!" He pointed at the column. "And the girl is you."

He took another bite from his bloody meal.

"And the baby?"

The Faun ignored the question.

"So," he said. "You retrieved the key." He bent forward until Ofelia saw her own reflection in his pale blue eyes. "I'm glad."

He straightened and held his hand out to the Fairy. She landed gracefully on his outstretched finger and the Faun chuckled with delight when she took a greedy bite from his meat.

"She believed in you from the beginning. And look at her! So happy!"

The Fairy fluttered off and the Faun followed her with his eyes as tenderly as a father watching his mischievous child. "She is so thrilled you succeeded!"

He laughed, but Ofelia saw his face was serious when he turned to her.

"Keep the key. You'll be needing it very soon." His long hand drew a warning into the night. He always accented his words with his fingers, stretching, pointing, drawing invisible signs, which seemed to reveal more than his tongue. "And this"—he handed Ofelia a piece of white chalk—"you will need as well! Two tasks remain and the moon will soon be full."

Ofelia couldn't help but shudder when he caressed her face with his clawed fingers.

"Be patient, Princess," he purred, smiling down at her. "We'll soon walk in the Seven Circular Gardens of your palace, stroll over its winding paths paved with onyx and alabaster . . ."

There was something mischievous in his cat eyes. Ofelia wasn't sure whether it had been there at their first meeting or whether she just hadn't noticed.

"How do I know that what you say is true?"

The Faun shook his horned head as if she'd deeply insulted him. "Why would a poor little faun like me lie to you?"

He traced the track of an invisible tear down his patterned cheek, but his eyes were those of a lurking cat, ready to pounce.

Ofelia stepped back, her heart pounding. Not with fear. No. Worse. She looked at the gold key in her hand—was it a treasure? Or a burden? She suddenly felt there was no one she could trust, no one in the world. Her mother had betrayed her to please the Wolf, and how could she ever come to believe she could trust the Faun?

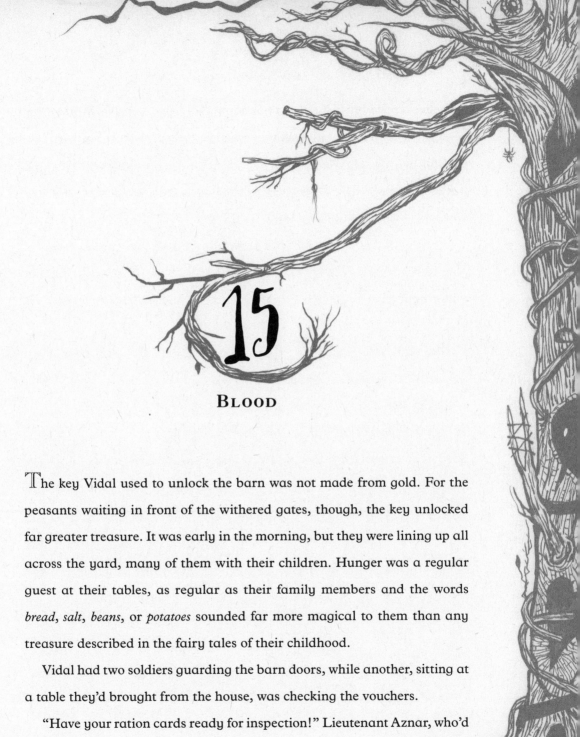

15

BLOOD

The key Vidal used to unlock the barn was not made from gold. For the peasants waiting in front of the withered gates, though, the key unlocked far greater treasure. It was early in the morning, but they were lining up all across the yard, many of them with their children. Hunger was a regular guest at their tables, as regular as their family members and the words *bread*, *salt*, *beans*, or *potatoes* sounded far more magical to them than any treasure described in the fairy tales of their childhood.

Vidal had two soldiers guarding the barn doors, while another, sitting at a table they'd brought from the house, was checking the vouchers.

"Have your ration cards ready for inspection!" Lieutenant Aznar, who'd been given the task to hand out the vouchers, barked the words with the confidence only a uniform can grant. He didn't know how it felt to wait in a line just to fill your empty stomach. He came from a butcher's family, and the worn figures with their tired faces and bent backs looked like an inferior species to him. For sure they were not his kind.

"Hurry up!" he barked at an old man, grabbing the voucher from his outstretched hand. "Your name. First and last." The lieutenant's butcher father had never looked like this old man. So exhausted, so marked by life.

"Narciso Peña Soriano . . . at your service," the old man said. They were all at their service. All their lives.

Aznar waved him into the barn.

"Name!" he called, and the line moved silently.

Mercedes and two other maids brought out baskets filled with fresh bread. Lieutenant Medem, who had brought all the treasure to the mill, held up one of the loaves of bread from Mercedes's basket.

"This is our daily bread in Franco's Spain!" his voice boomed across the yard. "Kept safe in this mill. The Reds lie when they tell you we let you starve. . . ."

Medem's words drifted up to the room Ofelia shared with her mother, waking her from a sleep heavy with dreams of the Faun and the Toad and the key that would unlock . . . what? Ofelia wasn't sure she wanted to know.

Words kept drifting in from outside.

". . . in a united Spain there is not a single home. . . ."

Ofelia slipped silently out of the bed so as to not wake her mother. Home . . .

". . . not a single home without fire or bread!"

Bread. The word made her hungry. So hungry. After all, she'd been sent to bed without supper after quite an exhausting adventure.

". . . not a single home without fire or bread." Even Ofelia knew that was a lie, though it was proclaimed with so much confidence. When do children realize that adults lie?

Was the Faun lying? He had looked even more sinister in Ofelia's dreams. *How do I know that what you say is true?* Her mother was moaning in her sleep and her face was glistening with sweat, although the sun hadn't warmed the house yet. She didn't wake when Ofelia tiptoed to the bathroom over the dusty floorboards spotted with morning light, but Ofelia locked the door nevertheless before she pulled the Faun's book from behind the radiator. Its pages were once again white as snow.

"Come on!" Ofelia whispered. "What happens next? Show me!"

And the book obeyed.

A speck of red appeared on the left-hand page. Another seeped through the page on the right. They both spread as fast as ink on wet paper. Red. Red running over the white pages, until it filled the crack between them and dripped onto Ofelia's bare feet.

She immediately knew what this meant, though she couldn't tell why. She raised her eyes from the book and stared at the door, behind which her mother was sleeping.

A muffled scream escaped the reddened pages.

Ofelia dropped the book and rushed to the door. She pushed it open to find her mother leaning heavily against the bed frame and pressing her hand against her belly. Her white nightgown was soaked in blood.

"O—Ofelia!" she stammered hoarsely, raising her hand pleadingly, her fingers red with her own blood. "Help me!"

Then she collapsed to the floor.

⁓⁄⁓

Vidal was in the yard, checking his watch, hiding its broken face with his black leather glove. How long it was taking to feed these peasants. So much time wasted just because one couldn't trust them. Vidal would have betted his uniform that some of them would take their provisions into the forest anyway to feed a relative or lover who'd joined the traitors. How he wished he could just break and kill them all like he had the rabbit poachers.

"*Capitán!*"

He turned around.

Had the girl lost her mind? She came running toward him in her nightgown. Usually she hid from him like a creature that knew it was best to stay invisible. Her mother wouldn't listen when he'd suggested to leave the girl for a while with her grandparents. That daughter was a weakness of hers and the only issue on which she dared to fight him, but he had no intention of raising a dead tailor's child.

Vidal's steps were stiff with anger as he walked toward the girl, but when he stopped in front of her he realized that the fear in Ofelia's face hadn't been caused by him.

"Come quickly!" she cried. "Please!"

Only then did Vidal notice the blood on her dress. It clearly wasn't the girl's. Fear stirred in the depth of his heart, fear and anger. Foolish woman. She would fail him and the child he gave her. He yelled at Serrano to get the doctor.

The sky had opened up and was once again soaking the world in rain. The perfect weather to match Dr. Ferreira's mood as he crossed the yard to report on his patient.

He found Vidal standing in front of the barn, staring at the tents and trucks he'd brought to the mill. To Ferreira they looked like abandoned toys against the fir trees looming above them. He put his jacket on. There was some blood on the sleeves.

"Your wife needs uninterrupted rest. She should be sedated most of the time until she gives birth." *You should never have brought her here*, he added in his mind. *You should never have made her daughter see her like this.* But instead he only said: "The girl should sleep somewhere else. I'll stay here until the child is born."

Vidal was still staring over the yard.

"Make her well," he said, without taking his eyes off the rain. "I don't care what it costs or what you need."

When he finally turned to Ferreira his face was rigid with anger. Anger at what? Ferreira wondered. At life? At himself for bringing his pregnant wife here? No. A man like Vidal never blamed himself. He was probably angry at the mother of his future child for proving herself to be so weak.

"Make her well," Vidal repeated. "Cure her."

It was an order. And a threat.

16

A Lullaby

The attic room Mercedes told the maids to turn into Ofelia's bedroom had a round window in the wall like the face of the full moon. But the room itself was even more desolate than the one Ofelia had shared with her mother, all its corners filled with stored-away boxes and furniture covered in ghostly shrouds yellowed by time and neglect.

"Would you like some supper?" asked Mercedes.

"No, thank you." Ofelia shook her head.

Mercedes had brought another maid to cover the bed with fresh sheets and pillows. The dark wood of the bed frame made the white fabrics look like snow. All the furniture at the mill was made from this kind of wood and for a moment Ofelia imagined the trees around the mill to rise and tear down its walls and take revenge for their brethren who'd been cut down to build beds and tables and chairs.

"You haven't eaten a thing," said Mercedes.

How could she eat? She was filled with sadness. Ofelia silently put her books on the bedside table and sat down on the blanket. White. Everything white would from now on remind her of red.

"Don't worry." Mercedes reached over the bed and touched Ofelia's shoulder. "Your mother will get better soon. You'll see. Having a baby is complicated."

"Then I'll never have one."

Ofelia hadn't cried since she'd found her mother soaked in blood, but Mercedes's soft voice made the tears finally run down her cheeks as densely as the blood had run over the pages of the Faun's book. Why hadn't the book warned her in time? Why show her something that was happening anyway? *Because the book is cruel*, something in Ofelia whispered, *as cruel as its cunning master. Even the Fairy is cruel.*

Yes, she was. Ofelia shuddered as she recalled the Fairy digging her teeth into the Faun's bloody meal. The Fairies in her books didn't have teeth like that, did they?

Mercedes sat down by her side and caressed Ofelia's hair. It was as black as her mother's. As black as coal, as white as snow, as red as blood . . .

"You're helping those men in the woods, aren't you?" Ofelia whispered.

Mercedes withdrew her hands.

"Have you told anyone?"

Ofelia saw that Mercedes didn't dare look at her.

"No, I haven't. I don't want anything bad to happen to you."

She leaned her head against Mercedes's shoulder and closed her eyes. She wanted to hide in her arms, from the world, from the blood, from the Wolf, from the Faun. There was no Underground Kingdom she could escape to. It was all lies. There was only one world and it was so dark.

Mercedes was not used to holding a child, although she was still young enough to have one. When she finally wrapped her arms around the girl, the softness stirring in her heart frightened her. It was dangerous to be soft in this world.

"And I don't want anything bad to happen to you!" she whispered back, cradling Ofelia in her arms, although part of her was still warning her of the tenderness she gave in to. She herself had once wished for a daughter, but the war had made her forget. It had made her forget many things.

"Do you know a lullaby?" Ofelia murmured.

Did she? Yes. . . .

"Only one. But I don't remember the words."

"I don't care. I still want to hear it." Ofelia looked up at her pleadingly.

So Mercedes closed her eyes and while she was gently rocking another woman's child in her arms, she began to hum the lullaby her mother had once sung to her and her brother. The wordless tune filled both her and the girl with the sweetness of love, like the first song ever sung on earth to the

105

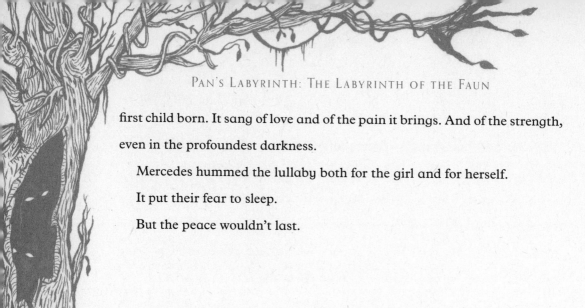

first child born. It sang of love and of the pain it brings. And of the strength, even in the profoundest darkness.

Mercedes hummed the lullaby both for the girl and for herself.

It put their fear to sleep.

But the peace wouldn't last.

17

BROTHER AND SISTER

Mercedes stayed with Ofelia until the girl fell asleep—finally, despite her worries about her mother, despite the fear that filled the old mill like the dust of black flour.

The house was silent when Mercedes stole down the stairs. Everyone was asleep, except for the guards outside. They were watching the forest and didn't see her kneel on the kitchen floor to wipe away the sand covering the tiles until she could lift one up. The bundle of letters she'd hidden underneath was still there, and so was the can filled with things she'd put aside for the men hiding in the forest. She was putting everything into her satchel when footsteps on the stairs made her freeze.

"It's only me, Mercedes," Dr. Ferreira whispered.

He came down the stairs slowly as if he were reluctant to finally do what he and Mercedes had planned to do for days.

"Are you ready?" *Please say yes*, Mercedes pleaded with her eyes. *I can't do this alone.*

Ferreira nodded.

Mercedes led the way. She walked through the brook to hide their tracks. Moonlight seeped through the trees and turned the water into melted silver.

"This is sheer madness," Ferreira muttered as the cold water filled his shoes. "If he finds out what we're doing, he'll kill us all." Of course, they both knew who he was talking about. "But I guess you thought about that?"

Had she thought of anything else?

Mercedes listened into the night. "Are you so afraid of him?"

Ferreira couldn't help but smile. She was so beautiful. Her courage was a royal cloak around her shoulders.

"No. It's not fear," he replied truthfully. "At least not for my—" He fell silent the moment Mercedes pressed her finger warningly against her lips.

Something was moving in the forest.

Mercedes gave a sigh of relief when a young man emerged from behind a tree as silently as the shadows the waxing moon painted onto the mossy ground. A dark cap covered his black hair and his clothes gave away that he'd clearly been in the woods for a while. Mercedes didn't take her eyes off him as he strode toward them through the ferns. Her brother was only a few years younger than she, but when they were children those years had made all the difference.

"Pedro!" She tenderly touched his beloved face when he stopped in front of her. Mercedes always forgot how tall he was.

Her brother gave her a long embrace. Once upon a time he had needed her protection only from the firm hand of their mother or his own reckless-ness, but these days it was far more dangerous to be a caring older sister. Sometimes Pedro wished that his older sister were less courageous and that she would take more care of herself. He'd even told her not to help them anymore, but Mercedes didn't care what others told her to do or not to do. His sister made her own rules. Mercedes always had, even as a child. He loved her very much.

THE WATCHMAKER

A long, long time ago, when most men measured their days by the sun, there ruled a king in Madrid who was obsessed with time and timepieces. He ordered hourglasses, clocks, watches, and sundials from famous clockmakers all over the world, paying for the delicate instruments by selling his subjects to other kings as soldiers or cheap field laborers. The halls of his palace were filled with the sound of sand running through huge hourglasses and even the sundials in his vast gardens counted the hours with the shadows they cast. He had clocks imitating his favorite birds and others announcing each full hour with the appearance of miniature knights and dragons. Even in the most remote corners of the world people called his royal palace in Madrid *El Palacio del Tiempo*, the Palace of Time.

The king's beautiful wife, Olvido, had borne him a son and a daughter, but they weren't allowed to play and laugh like other children. Their days were measured and ruled by the clocks the king had given them, ordering them, with their silver and gold dials, when to rise and eat and play and sleep.

One day the king's favorite fool dared to joke that his master was only obsessed with timepieces because he was afraid of death and hoped that by measuring time he could keep it away.

The king was not a man who forgave easily. The next day his soldiers chained the fool to the cogwheels of his largest clock and the king watched without a hint of compassion as the wheels broke every bone in his former favorite's body. As hard as they tried, the servants couldn't wash all the blood from the cogwheels and the clock was henceforth called the Red Clock, people whispering that its ticking repeated the dead fool's name.

The years went by. The prince and princess grew up and the king's collection of clocks was envied all over the world. Then one day—it was approaching the tenth anniversary of the fool's execution—a gift arrived at the palace from an unknown sender. In a box made of glass lay a beautiful pocket watch. Its silver coat case was open, showing the king's initials engraved inside the lid and two lean silver dials moving from minute to minute, their ticking as subtle as the footsteps of a dragonfly.

When the king took the watch from the box, he found a carefully folded and sealed piece of paper underneath. He turned pale as he read the message, which was written in a firm and beautiful hand:

Your Majesty,

When this watch stops, you will die. It knows the exact hour, minute, and second, for I have locked your Death inside. Don't try to break it. The end of your life will only arrive faster.

The Watchmaker

The king stared at the watch in his hand. He felt as if the dials were stabbing his heart with every second they measured. He couldn't move. He could no longer eat or drink or go to sleep. His hair and beard turned gray in a matter of days, and all he could do was continue to stare at the watch.

The prince sent his father's soldiers out to find the messenger who had delivered the deadly gift. They found him in a nearby village but the man didn't know the watchmaker's name. He swore he'd received the box at a deserted mill in the old forest but when he led them there, the king's soldiers found only an abandoned workshop. The shelves and workbenches were empty except for a small silver figurine of a dancing fool. It was standing in a bowl of blood. The soldiers rushed back to the castle to report their findings. But they were too late. The king was dead, still sitting on his throne, the pocket watch clenched in his cold hand. The watch had stopped at exactly the same hour, minute, and second that the fool had died.

Only then did the prince remember that the fool had also had a son.

18

THE SECOND TASK

This time Ofelia did not wake from Fairy wings buzzing in the dark. For a moment the sound piercing her dreams made her wonder whether the forest had come into her room. But when she sat up, the Faun was standing at the foot of her bed, his limbs creaking like the branches of an old tree in the wind.

"You didn't carry out the next task yet," he growled.

He once again looked different. Stronger. Younger . . . reminding Ofelia of a very annoyed lion this time, with his catlike eyes, his perfectly rounded ears, and his long pale-yellow hair, which looked more and more like a mane. Lion, goat, man, he was all of it and none. He was . . . the Faun.

"I couldn't!" Ofelia defended herself. "My mother is sick! Very sick!"

"That's no excuse for negligence!" the Faun snarled, his hands writing his anger into the night. "Well . . . ," he added after a pause. "I'll forgive you for now. And I brought something that will help your mother."

The pale lumpy root he held up was bigger than his fist and it looked to Ofelia as if it were spreading twisted arms and legs. Like a baby frozen in mid-birth scream.

"This is a mandrake root," the Faun explained, handing the strange thing to Ofelia. "A plant that dreamt of being human. Put it under your mother's bed in a fresh bowl of milk, and feed it each morning with two drops of blood."

Ofelia disliked the scent of the root as much as its strangely human shape. It resembled a baby born with nothing but a mouth. And without hands and feet.

"Now! No more delays. No time to waste!" The Faun clapped his hands. "The full moon will be upon us. Ah yes." He removed his wooden satchel. "I almost forgot! You'll need my pets to guide you."

Ofelia heard the Fairy chattering inside as he put the satchel on her blanket.

"Yes. You're going to a very dangerous place." The Faun lifted a warning finger, the lines on his forehead swirling like whirls in a bottomless river. "Far more dangerous than the last one. So be careful!"

For a moment he sounded sincerely worried about her.

"The thing that slumbers in that place—" He shook his horned head and frowned with disgust. "It is not human, although it may look like it. It's very old and full of cunning and cruelty—and a great hunger."

He plucked a big hourglass out of the air and dropped it on Ofelia's bed.

"Here. You'll need this, too. You'll see a sumptuous banquet, but don't eat or drink anything. Nothing!" This time both hands drew a warning sign into the night. "Absolutely nothing!"

Ofelia looked at the objects on her blanket: the mandrake root, the satchel, the hourglass. Three gifts . . . just like the heroes in her fairy tales often received. These gifts always proved to be very helpful—unless one lost them or used them the wrong way.

"Ab-so-lute-ly nothing!" the Faun repeated, his clawed fingers piercing the night. "Your life will depend on it."

And before Ofelia could ask him to tell her more, he was gone.

19

A Cave in the Woods

The rebels had found shelter in a cave about half an hour's walk from the mill. The trees hid it well and there was just enough room for the dozen men and their belongings: a few bundles of ragged clothes, a pile of tattered books, and blankets far too thin to keep the cold away, the last remnants of lives these men had left behind because they couldn't say yes to marching boots and Franco's clean Spain. To choose freedom comes with a high price.

"I've brought some Orujo." Mercedes took the bottle of Vidal's favorite liquor out of her satchel. "And tobacco and cheese. And there's mail."

The men who had received letters took the envelopes with shaking hands.

117

As they walked into the back of the cave to read what their loved ones had written, some of the others sniffed longingly at the cheese Mercedes had stolen. The aroma took them back to better times when they'd made their own cheese from their own goats and freedom had not been a luxury to pay for with fear and misery.

The patient Mercedes had brought Ferreira along for was lying on an old cot, reading a tattered book, his head propped on a sleeping bag. The others called him Frenchie and his eyeglasses were the most valuable thing he'd had been able to save of his former belongings. He didn't look up from his book when Dr. Ferreira bent over his bandaged leg.

"How do you think it's doing?" he asked Ferreira. "I'll lose it, right?"

The doctor took off his jacket and rolled up his sleeves. "Let's see."

Ferreira drew comfort from his profession in these dark times: he liked being a healer when most others embraced destruction, but even healing had become a deadly task. The man he'd come to help had sentenced himself to death by joining the men in the woods, and Ferreira knew he was accepting the same sentence for himself by helping the rebels.

He hesitated for a moment before he removed the bloodstained bandage. Even after all these years, he couldn't get used to the fact he often needed to cause pain to help. Managing to suppress a groan, Frenchie shuddered when the bandage came off and Ferreira wondered how many of these men in the woods regretted joining a fight that looked more and more like a lost cause.

Mercedes had brought a newspaper and Pedro's friend Tarta delivered some distraction for them all by reading aloud from it. No one knew why Tarta's tongue couldn't form words without breaking them into fragments. In Ferreira's experience a stutter bore witness to a skin too thin to keep the darkness of the world at bay. The soft and sensible ones developed it, the ones who couldn't help but see and feel it all. Tarta still looked like a boy, always wearing a hint of melancholy on his gentle face, his dark eyes gazing at the world with wonder and bewilderment.

"'British and C-C-Canadian troops disembarked on a small beach in the North of F-Fr . . .'"

"France, you idiot," one of the others snapped, grabbing the newspaper, hiding his own fears of what news it would bring behind cruelty and anger.

"'More than 150,000 soldiers give us hope,'" he read.

Hope . . . Ferreira looked at Frenchie's shattered leg. A bullet had done the damage, of course. Bullet wounds were a far-too-familiar sight to the doctor by now and this one looked terrible. Luckily the old man couldn't see the damage. *Old?* Ferreira mocked himself. Frenchie was probably his age.

"'Under the command of General Dwight D. Eisenhower . . .'"

Frenchie gasped the moment Ferreira touched his leg. "Is it as bad as I think?"

"Look, Frenchie . . ." Ferreira's voice was soft with compassion. He took off his glasses in a vain attempt to see things less clearly for a moment. "There is no way to save this leg."

The cave filled with silence. And the wounded man's fear.

119

The others surrounded Frenchie as Ferreira opened his bag. At least he had his tools thanks to the fact he also treated the soldiers who'd done this. But he had no anesthetic.

Mercedes made Frenchie drink half the bottle of Vidal's liquor; not much comfort for a man who was about to have his leg sawed off.

"I'll do this as quickly as I can with as few cuts as possible." Ferreira wished he could've have made a less pathetic promise.

Frenchie nodded and grabbed Mercedes's hand. Though not a mother, she played the role for the second time tonight—first for Ofelia, now for a man she barely knew. Mother, sister, wife . . . Mercedes was the only woman the men in the woods had seen in a long time and for some she played all these parts. Like most of the men, she shut her eyes when Ferreira pressed his bone saw against Frenchie's swollen leg.

"Wait a second, Doctor! Just a second."

Frenchie gazed one more time at his leg. His choice to fight the marching boots would make him a cripple. Ferreira wondered how that made him feel about his decision. Frenchie inhaled deeply, pressing his lips firmly together, as if that would keep the screams inside, the screams, the despair, the fear . . . then he nodded again.

This time it was Ferreira who had to catch his breath, to pull himself together for the butchery he was about to perform. Sometimes even the healers are turned into butchers by the darkness of this world.

120

20

THE PALE MAN

In Ofelia's attic room, there was no need to hide the Faun's book. She kept it on her nightstand where only its size made it stand out among the other books. The maids pitied her for being banished to the attic—Ofelia saw it in their faces when they brought her meals. But Ofelia actually didn't mind. It had gotten harder and harder to sleep next to her mother, whose labored breathing and distress made her so angry at her unborn brother that at times when she tried to imagine what he'd look like she gave him his father's face.

She first could barely make her fingers open the book. The memory of the blood dripping off its pages haunted her, but her wish to know about

121

her next task was stronger than her fear. The Faun had taught her his first lesson: she knew about her courage since she'd crawled through the Toad's endless tunnels. And this time she'd put on the coat to make sure for the next task she wore something that kept her warm and wouldn't be ruined in case it got dirty.

The book revealed its secrets more quickly than before. The left-hand page filled first, fine lines revealing the skeletal figure of a pale man, noseless and bald, with holes instead of eyes above a gaping mouth. The brown ink drew a Fairy, then a door. The image took shape in more and more detail while Ofelia read the words appearing on the right-hand page:

Use the chalk to trace a door anywhere in your room.

Chalk. Ofelia reached into her coat pocket for the piece of chalk the Faun had given her. For a moment she was afraid she'd lost it, but finally her fingers found it. The image in the book was still unfolding. The girl in the green dress and white apron appeared beneath the Pale Man, in clothes as clean as if Ofelia had never ruined them in the woods. The three Fairies were by her side. The girl smiled out at Ofelia. Then she knelt with the chalk in her hand and drew the outline of a door onto the wall. And more words appeared:

Once the door is open, start the hourglass and let the Fairy guide you. . . .

The open door now framed by a stone arch was held by two columns that took shape beneath the Pale Man's right arm.

Don't eat or drink anything during your stay,

the words on the right page warned,

and come back before the last grain of sand falls.

More images were forming, but Ofelia found it by now all far too much to remember, so she closed the book and knelt with the chalk as the girl in the illustration had done. The attic wall was covered in spiderwebs and quite uneven, but the chalk left a clear line on the plaster. It turned into white foam and, hissing softly, etched a door into the wall that gave way like the gate to an ancient tomb, when Ofelia pressed her hand against it. The opening behind it was so narrow that she had to bend her back to gaze through. She looked down into a wide corridor, its ceiling high above her head and the floor at least seven feet below her. Columns lined it with walls as dark red as dried blood. Shafts of light fell through small windows onto the white-and-brownish-red-checkered tile floor.

As it was too far down to jump, Ofelia got a chair from the attic and lowered it through the opening. Then she slung the Faun's satchel over her shoulder and placed the hourglass on the floor next to her bed. As soon as

Ofelia turned it over, a small amount of pale red sand began to fill worryingly fast into the lower glass.

The chair served her well as a ladder. When Ofelia jumped from it onto the checkered floor she heard a wheezing sound in the distance . . . as if someone were breathing heavily in sleep. The sound mingled with the echoing of her footsteps as she followed the corridor, which seemed to wind on and on like a river, the columns casting shadows onto the tiles like an endless row of petrified trees. Ofelia felt as if she had been walking for hours when the corridor suddenly opened up into a dark, windowless room.

For a moment Ofelia wondered whether she'd been lost in time and was back in a long-forgotten past. The room looked so ancient under its painted ceiling, but Ofelia didn't look at the faded images above her head. All she saw was the long table at the center of the room. It was covered with golden bowls and plates filled to the brim with fruits, cakes, and roasted meats, but only the chair at the very end of the table was taken. The Pale Man sat on it, illuminated by the flames dancing in the fireplace behind him.

He didn't move when Ofelia approached the table. In fact, he looked as if he hadn't moved for centuries, whereas the food looked as fresh as if it had just been prepared. Ofelia couldn't take her eyes off all the cakes, puddings, and roasts decorated with fruit and edible flowers, the golden plates reflecting in crystal goblets filled with red wine. Red and gold . . . the whole room was filled with those colors, even the flames echoed them. And the heavenly aromas! They made Ofelia forget everything, even the frightening creature sitting so silently just a few feet away from her in front of his plate.

Only when she reached his end of the table did she remember him. Seeing him up close made her gasp. He was naked, just as the book had shown, his pale skin loosely covering his bones like an ill-fitting shroud. It was a horrible sight, but the worst was his face. Or the lack of one.

The creature's face was an obscene blank, marred only by two nostrils and a razor-thin mouth—a bloodstained slit framed by heavy folds of sagging skin—and his clawed hands, lying motionless beside his golden plate, ended in pointed black fingertips, the flesh above them reddened by blood.

The fact the monster didn't move made Ofelia bold. She peered over his plate between the terrible hands, curious why it held two marbles, and withdrew hastily when she discovered the marbles to be eyeballs. Only then did she give the images on the ceiling a closer look. What they revealed made Ofelia back away from the table despite all the delicacies it held: the images above her showed the Pale Man's profession.

Some images depicted children raising their hands and pleading for mercy. Others showed the monster piercing them with knives and swords, or tearing off their limbs or feeding his insatiable hunger with their flesh. The scenes were painted so vividly Ofelia believed she could hear the victims scream. Too much! But when she lowered her eyes to escape the grueling images all she saw were hundreds of small shoes piled against the walls.

Ofelia could barely make herself face the truth, but there it was. The Pale Man was a Child Eater.

Yes, he was.

But if he eats children . . . why all the food? Ofelia wondered. *Why the luxurious feast?*

She could find the answer neither in the terrible images above her nor among the golden plates. All she had to do, she reminded herself of the book's advice, was to stay away from the table and let the Fairies help her. The three Fairies greeted her with a pleased twitter when she opened the satchel. Ignoring the grueling host at the table, they fluttered to the left side of the room, where high up in the wall a set of three small doors was surrounded by carvings of gaping mouths, staring eyes, and flames, above an image of a labyrinth.

The doors were barely larger than Ofelia's hand and each one looked slightly different—but all three Fairies pointed to the door in the middle. It was beautiful—shiny and covered in gold.

Ofelia took the Toad's key out of her pocket, but suddenly she remembered what the stories in her fairy-tale books had taught her: *When faced with three choices, always choose the least obvious choice. The humble one.*

"Oh, you're wrong!" she whispered to the Fairy. "This is not the right door!"

And paying no heed to their irritated chatter, Ofelia tried the key in the lock on the humblest door made from rustic wood and iron nails. The key slipped in effortlessly. Ofelia gave her winged companions a triumphant look before she opened the tiny door. The Fairies, though, hearing the red sand running through the hourglass, swarmed around her, urging her to make haste.

The compartment behind the door was deep, almost too deep for Ofelia to reach what was hidden inside. Finally, she touched soft fabrics and cool metal. The object she pulled out was wrapped in red velvet, and Ofelia almost dropped it when she realized what she held in her hands.

It was a dagger, its long blade as silvery as the moonlight, its golden handle embossed with the image of a faun.

And a baby.

The Fairies once again swarmed around Ofelia, urging her to hurry, but it was so hard for her to remember the running sand in this ancient room where everything seemed frozen in time, including the pale-skinned Child Eater. One of the Fairies, making sure the monster was still not moving, came so close to the terrible face her wings almost brushed his skin, but the Child Eater remained motionless, as if he were only his own monument, a memorial of all his horrible deeds.

Ofelia put the dagger into the Faun's satchel and tried to keep her eyes on the Pale Man while she walked back to the table. All the food looked so delicious. She couldn't remember when she'd last seen such a cake or such fresh fruit. *Never!* And she was hungry. *Truly hungry,* her heart whispered as she raised her hand. *Don't eat or drink anything!* But Ofelia saw the grapes and pomegranates and foods she didn't even know by name. They all promised such delicious sweetness she didn't want to hear the panicked warnings being chirped by the Fairies.

No. Ofelia waved them away. One grape—just one. Surely nobody would notice in this abundant feast. Who would miss a single little grape?

Ofelia gingerly plucked one grape and put it into her mouth. The Fairy who'd met her in the woods covered her face in despair.

They were doomed.

The Pale Man came to life. His black fingertips, pointy like thorns, cracked into motion with a spasm. His gaping mouth drew a tortured breath, and his right hand grabbed one of the eyeballs from his plate in his right hand, as his left turned, spreading its fingers like a terrible flower. The eyeball fit perfectly into the hole gaping in his left palm, and when his right hand had received the second eyeball, with a pupil as red as the grape Ofelia had eaten, the Pale Man raised both hands to his eyeless face to find out who had woken him.

Ofelia hadn't noticed what she'd done. The enchantment the table offered was too strong and the Fairy that had brought her to the labyrinth couldn't stop her from plucking another of the treacherous grapes.

Oh, that girl!

Why did she make it so difficult to help her? Their horned master would be so angry. The Fairy fluttered right in front of the girl's face to break the spell, even managing to pull the grape from her fingers. But was the child grateful? Oh no. Ofelia was angry. *Don't they understand?* she thought, yanking the grape back from the Fairy. All she wished was to drown herself in sweetness, to have the fruit make her forget everything—all the bitterness, all the pain, and all the fear that filled her life.

The Pale Man had risen from his chair. He stepped out from behind the table, his legs moving as stiffly as if they'd forgotten how to carry his skeletal body. He kept his hands raised to his face, the eyes in his palms

searching for the thief who'd woken him and stolen from his table.

First those eyes found the Fairies.

And then Ofelia.

Who still didn't notice what she had done.

Oh, how the Fairies were screaming now. But their voices were barely louder than the chirping of crickets and Ofelia bit into another grape while the Pale Man came closer, his skin hanging from his bony limbs like clothes sewn from flesh. The Fairies swarmed around the Child Eater's terrible head, desperate to distract him from the girl. Their fear made their voices so shrill they finally pierced through the enchantment.

Ofelia turned, but it was too late. The Child Eater was grasping for the Fairies with his bloodstained fingers. First, they managed to escape, but the Pale Man was an experienced hunter. The two he caught fought desperately for their lives, but their captor wouldn't let go and Ofelia had to watch the monster stuff the first Fairy between his toothless gums. He tore off her head as effortlessly as plucking a flower from its stem, her blood running down his pale chin. The second Fairy, struggling helplessly against his cruel grip, met the same fate as her sister, her wings and limbs crushed between the colorless lips. The Pale Man was licking her blood off his fingers when Ofelia finally managed to make her feet move.

She ran out into the corridor but soon heard the Pale Man's unsteady steps behind her. When she looked back, she saw his terrible figure between the columns, his eyes darting restlessly in his raised hands. *Run!* Ofelia told her feet. *Run!* But her knees were trembling and she slipped and fell onto the checkered floor.

The last Fairy, the one who had survived, fluttered to Ofelia's side. *Your sisters are dead because of me!* Ofelia thought, stumbling on. No. She couldn't think about that now. She still couldn't see the end of the corridor and up in the attic room the sand was running through the Faun's hourglass.

Maybe it was good Ofelia couldn't see how little sand was left. Her heart was racing when she reached the last bend in the corridor. There was the chair and above it the door the chalk had cut.

But the Fairy heard the sand running.

Ofelia was just two steps away from the chair when the door above it slowly began to close.

"No!" Ofelia screamed. "No!"

Gasping, she scrambled onto the chair, but when she reached up, the door was gone and it wouldn't come back, although she beat her fists against the wall. What made her feverish mind remember the chalk? Maybe the Fairy reminded her with a whisper?

Ofelia searched the Faun's satchel.

Nothing.

Searching her coat pocket, she was more successful.

The Pale Man's steps echoed louder and louder through the corridor, and Ofelia's fingers were so tense with fear she broke the chalk in two. She could barely keep a grip on the small piece left in her hand.

Behind her the Pale Man stepped around the corner. He lifted his right hand to stare at Ofelia. There she was. Oh, he loved when they tried to escape. It was as much about the hunt as it was about the kill.

The Fairy twittered in terror, but she didn't leave Ofelia's side when

Ofelia climbed onto the back of the chair to reach the ceiling.

Closer. The Pale Man staggered closer and closer, stalking on his skeleton legs, his eyes glinting in his palms.

Ofelia finally managed to draw a square onto the mosaics covering the ceiling. She pushed against the door with all the strength she had left and finally the chalk outline gave way, but when Ofelia pulled herself up, hoping this door would also lead back to her room, her feet lost hold of the chair. The Fairy flitted past her as Ofelia struggled to drag her body up and away from the terrible hands. The Pale Man's fingernails brushed her legs, but as he used his hands to catch Ofelia he was blind and she finally managed to drag herself onto the dusty floor of the attic room. She pushed the trapdoor the chalk had cut back into place until only a fine line of light gave away the opening that had saved her.

Ofelia got to her feet.

A groan echoed through the floor, the moaning of a hungry blood-stained mouth, and when she stepped back, she felt the Pale Man pushing against the floorboards. The worst fears are always underneath us, hidden, shaking the ground we wish to be firm and safe.

Trembling, Ofelia sat down on her bed to get her feet off the floor, and listened. When the Fairy landed on her shoulder, the warmth of her small body was both comfort and accusation. After all, Ofelia's failings had killed her sisters.

A last brutal blow came from below.

And then . . . finally . . . silence.

21

No Choice

The day had barely broken when Pedro brought Mercedes and Dr. Ferreira back to the clearing near the brook where he'd picked them up. He was all confidence with the morning light on his face and the air fresh with the promise of new beginnings.

"We'll soon have reinforcements from Jaca! Fifty men or more." There was neither doubt nor fear in his voice, despite the despair they'd all seen last night on Frenchie's face. "As soon as they arrive, we'll go head-to-head with Vidal."

Ferreira had seen this before: the enthusiasm a new day could bring after even the darkest night. Sometimes it was strong enough to last, but most times it died by dusk. Ferreira himself had not yet recovered from taking Frenchie's leg. All that pain, the despair of the wounded man and

132

his comrades, his own helplessness . . .

"Head-to-head and then what?" he couldn't help asking. "You'll kill Vidal and they'll send another just like him. And another after that . . ."

Ferreira had witnessed too many failed hopes in his life. Had he really just lived for forty-eight years? He felt a thousand years old, and he was tired of all these young men who wished to fight, even if they did so on the side of right.

Pedro didn't bother to answer his question. Mercedes's brother just looked at him, with his fresh young face. What did he see? Probably just a sad old man.

"You can't win this!" Ferreira snapped. "You don't have enough guns, no safe shelter! You'll all end up like Frenchie. Or worse." He knelt at the edge of the brook to wash the blood off his saw and scalpel. For sure he would need these tools again far too soon. The cold water rushed over his hands. As cold as the world.

"You don't need more men," he said. "The ones you have need food! And medicine!"

Pedro still hadn't said a word. Behind them the rebels were collecting firewood and whatever else the forest could give them.

"America, Russia, England . . . they'll all help us," he finally said. "Once they win the big war against the German fascists they'll help us beat them here in Spain. Franco supported Hitler, but we supported the allies. Many of us died helping the resistance; we sabotaged the Tungsten mines in Galicia, which the Germans need to keep their weapon factories running . . . you think the allies will forget that?"

Ferreira straightened and put his tools back into his bag. Yes, they *would* forget. He felt so tired and angry. Maybe his anger was mostly caused by his exhaustion and lack of hope. *And don't forget the fear*, he told himself. Fear that the good causes never win—that they can only hold up evil for a while.

"What about Mercedes?" No, even though he was annoyed by his own voice, he couldn't let it go. "If you really loved her, you'd cross the border with her. This is a lost cause!"

Pedro bent his head, as if he were listening to his heart to find out if part of it agreed. Then he looked at Ferreira again.

"I am staying here, Doctor," he said. "There is no choice."

His voice was as determined as his face. Not a trace of doubt or fear.

We feel immortal when we are young. Or maybe we just don't care that much about death yet?

As Pedro left to find his sister, Ferreira followed the young guerrilla with his eyes. Had he ever been like this? he asked himself. No. Or maybe yes. When he was still a boy and the world was black-and-white and there was good and evil. When had the world become less simple? Or was this just the perception of his exhausted heart?

Mercedes was picking berries while her brother talked to Ferreira. The forest offered so much to those who honored it. The woods had never frightened Mercedes, even when she was so little her mother had tried to make her fear it by telling her tales of living trees, watermen, and witches. For her the forest had always meant shelter, nourishment, and life . . . she was not surprised that it now protected her brother. Pedro looked so grown-up by

134

now. As if he was the older one. Maybe by now he was, Mercedes thought, when she saw him walking toward her.

"Sister, you have to leave."

He put his hands on her shoulders. The gesture betrayed the emotions his voice managed to hide. Mercedes reached into her pocket and handed him the key to the barn. She'd stolen it the day before from the *capitán*'s drawer while cleaning his room.

"Wait a few more days," she cautioned. "If you raid the barn now, it will be exactly what he expects."

Her brother took the key with a triumphant smile. For a moment he didn't look grown-up at all, but like the eager boy Mercedes remembered so well. "Don't worry. Leave it to me. I'll be careful." He put his arm around her shoulders and kissed her cheek.

Careful. He was never careful. He didn't know the meaning of the word. Mercedes grabbed his hand, prolonging the precious moment. That's what kept them all alive: stealing moments.

"I am a coward," she whispered.

The surprise on Pedro's face almost made her smile.

"No, you're not!"

"Yes, I am. A coward . . . for living next to that beast of a man, doing his laundry, making his bed, feeding him. . . .What if the doctor is right and we can't win?"

Pedro paused. Finally, he nodded, as if to acknowledge that possibility.

"Then at least we'll make things harder for that evil son of a bitch," he said.

The Razor and the Knife

In a hut in the old forest there once lived a woman named Rocio, whom the people of the surrounding villages called a witch. She had a son and a daughter from a man she had left after he used his belt on the children.

"I may have to leave you soon," she said to them just a few days after her son had celebrated his twelfth birthday and her daughter was two months away from turning eleven. "I saw my death last night in my dreams. I am not afraid to go to the Underground Kingdom, but I am worried you two may be too young to deal with this world on your own. So I will give you both gifts that will keep you safe in case my dream comes true."

The children exchanged a frightened glance. Their mother's dreams always came true.

Rocio held her daughter's hand and closed the girl's fingers around the smooth wooden handle of a small kitchen knife.

"This blade will protect you from all harm, Luisa," the witch said. "And it will do more. This knife cuts through the masks of men and reveals the true faces they so often try to hide."

Luisa had to hold back her tears, as she loved her mother very much, but she took the knife and hid it in the folds of her apron.

"For you, Miguel, I have a different kind of blade," the witch said to her son, closing his fingers around the silver handle of a razor. "This will serve you as well as the kitchen knife will serve your sister. Its blade will protect you from all harm with its sharp bite, and when you grow old enough to shave, this razor will not only remove stubble from your chin, but it'll also rid you of painful memories. Each time you use it will make your heart feel as young as a freshly shaven face. Be careful, though. Some memories we have to keep, though they cut deep. Use my gift therefore wisely, my son, and not too often."

The next day Rocio didn't return from the part of the forest where she gathered fresh herbs each day. Only the following morning did her children learn that a nobleman had ordered his soldiers to drown her in the millpond where she'd often taken them to ask the water about the past and the future.

Knowing the children of a witch were rarely kept alive, Luisa and Miguel hastily packed what little they owned and left the hut they called home. They found a cave on the other side of the forest, a safe distance from the mill where their mother had died. It granted them shelter from the rain and the sharp teeth of the night, and the two blades gave them food and even protected them from the Pale Man when he one day roamed the forest close to their cave.

The air already smelled of snow when a farmer poaching rabbits in the forest found them. As he and his wife were unable to have children, he took them home without asking where they came from, and the childless couple loved and raised them as their own. When they grew up, Luisa became a kitchen maid and Miguel learned to be a barber, and the two blades their mother had given to them continued to feed and protect them.

Luisa and Miguel treasured their mother's gifts all their lives and when, many years later, they passed these gifts on to their children, both the knife and the razor were still as sharp and shiny as when Rocio had first put them in her children's hands. As they both had only daughters, the razor was passed to Miguel's son-in-law, whose heart was dark and cruel. One day in a fit of anger he pressed the blade to his wife's throat. The razor wouldn't obey him and cut his hand instead, but from that day onward, instead of removing painful memories, the razor blade brought them back for the men who used it, and poisoned them with their own darkness.

22

THE KINGDOMS OF DEATH AND LOVE

Vidal hadn't slept well, and while he scraped his freshly washed skin with the razor, he caught himself hoping the blade would rid him of both his dark stubble and the troubling dreams that were still nesting in the shadows the morning painted in the dusty room.

The shaving cream turned the water as white as milk as it washed off the blade. Why did that remind him of his unborn son and his bleeding wife? Next to the bowl lay the pocket watch ticking away his life. *Death!* the silver dials seemed to warn. Maybe death was the only love in Vidal's heart. His greatest romance. Nothing compared to it. So grand, so absolute, a celebration of darkness, of finally giving in completely. Even in death, though,

140

there was of course the fear of failing, of fading away unnoticed and with-out glory, face in the dirt—or worse, ending up like his mother, in bed, sickness eating away at her body. Women died like that. Not men.

Vidal stared at his reflection. The remaining shaving cream made it look as if his flesh was already rotting. He lifted the razor so close to the glass the blade seemed to slit his throat. Was there fear in his eyes?

No.

He abruptly dropped his hand, summoning the mask of confidence that had become his second face, merciless, determined. Death is a lover to be feared and there was only one way to overcome that fear—by being her executioner.

Maybe Vidal all alone in front of the mirror, courting her with his razor, sensed that Death had come to the mill. Maybe he heard her silent footsteps on the stairs to the room where his pregnant wife was tossing restlessly in bedding drenched with sweat.

Ofelia heard Death's footsteps too. She was standing by her mother's bed caressing her face. It was as hot as if life were being burned to ashes inside her. Was her unborn brother afraid too? Ofelia laid her hand on the curve his tiny body made under the blankets. Did he feel the heat of his mother's fever on his tiny face? Ofelia was tired of being angry with him. It was this place that made her mother sick, not him—and the only one to be blamed was the Wolf. In fact, she caught herself yearning to have her brother for company, to hold him and take care of him the way the girl carved in the column in the labyrinth took care of the child in her arms.

141

Sometimes we need to see what we feel so we can know about it.

Ofelia had come to her mother's room to do as the Faun had told her. She'd brought a bowl of milk and the mandrake he'd given her, although the root still disgusted her. It began to stir the moment it touched the milk, stretching its pale limbs like a newborn. Its arms and legs were as chubby as a baby's; even the noises it made resembled the muffled squeals of a newborn. And when Ofelia's mother moaned in her bed, the mandrake turned like a child toward the sound, as though listening for its mother's voice.

Ofelia had to smile despite her disgust. It kept squealing softly as she carried the bowl over to the bed. It wasn't easy placing the bowl underneath without spilling the milk. Ofelia had to crawl under the bed to push the bowl out of sight and for a moment she was worried the mandrake would wake her mother as it started crying like a baby. A hungry baby. Of course! Ofelia bit into her finger and pressed it until two drops of blood spilled into the milk. Only then, as she lay under the bed, did she hear footsteps.

Someone came in and stood by her mother's bed. Ofelia was relieved to recognize Dr. Ferreira's shoes.

But Ferreira hadn't come alone.

"*Capitán!*" Ofelia heard him say. "Her temperature is down! I don't know how, but it is."

Ferreira was very relieved. Since the girl had found her mother bleeding, he'd been worried she'd soon be an orphan and that they would lose her unborn brother as well. Ferreira had tried his best to hide these worries from Ofelia, but he had seen the fear in her eyes, eyes as dark as her mother's. And he knew he wouldn't be able to protect the girl from the man standing by his side, if her mother died. The girl who was lying under her mother's bed, her heart racing . . .

"So? She still has a fever." Ofelia heard neither relief nor worry in the Wolf's voice. Or love.

"Yes, but that's a good sign," she heard the doctor say. "Her body is responding to my treatment."

Ofelia felt her mother moving in her sleep above her.

"Listen to me, Ferreira. . . ." The Wolf's voice was so cold. "If you have to choose, save the baby. Understood?"

Ofelia couldn't breathe. Her heart was screaming. Each word the Wolf uttered was a slap in her mother's feverish face.

"That boy," he continued, "will bear my name. And my father's name. Save him. If he—"

A sudden explosion silenced him. Ofelia was sure it came from the forest. Death was not only inside the mill.

When Vidal stumbled out of the house, he found his soldiers gathered in the yard. A fireball was rising from the canopy of the trees, painting gray smoke into the sky.

Ofelia heard two more explosions when she crawled out from under the bed. She didn't care. Her mother's face was peaceful for the first time since her nightgown had been soaked with blood, and Ofelia gently pressed her ear against her mother's pregnant belly.

"Brother!" she whispered. "Little brother, if you can hear me, things out here aren't too good. But soon you'll have to come out."

She was so tired of the tears, but they filled her eyes nevertheless.

"You've made Mamá very sick."

If you have to choose, save the baby. The Wolf's words brought back her anger, but Ofelia didn't want it. From now on it would be the three of them against him. Mother, sister, brother. That's how it had to be.

"I want to ask you one favor!" she pleaded. "For when you come out. Just one. Please don't hurt her."

Ofelia's tears painted wet spots on her mother's blanket, as if all the sadness and fear she felt had become liquid. "You'll see when you meet her," she said. "Mamá's very pretty, even though she's sometimes sad for many days. And when she smiles . . . I know you'll love her. I'm sure you will!"

There was no answer, but Ofelia believed she heard her brother's heart beating underneath her mother's skin.

"Listen!" She gave her words all the weight a solemn promise needs. "If you do what I say, I'll take you to my kingdom and I'll make you a prince. I promise! A prince."

Underneath the bed the mandrake uttered a soft squeal.

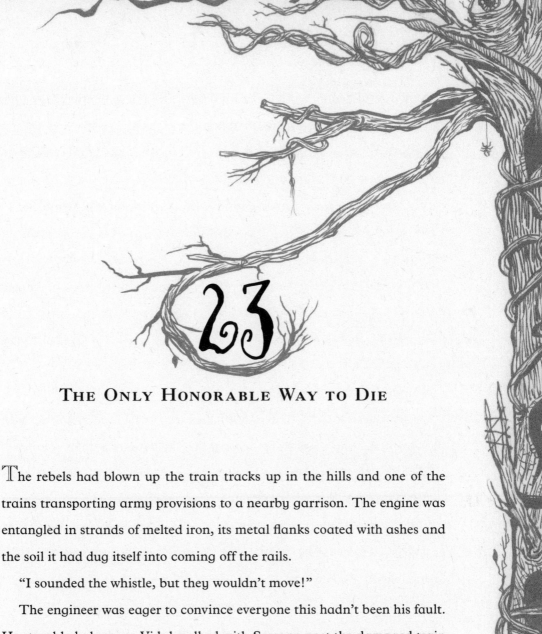

23

The Only Honorable Way to Die

The rebels had blown up the train tracks up in the hills and one of the trains transporting army provisions to a nearby garrison. The engine was entangled in strands of melted iron, its metal flanks coated with ashes and the soil it had dug itself into coming off the rails.

"I sounded the whistle, but they wouldn't move!"

The engineer was eager to convince everyone this hadn't been his fault. He stumbled along, as Vidal walked with Serrano past the damaged train cars.

"I tried to stop! I swear! But it was too late."

Idiot. Only the guilty ones talk that fast. Vidal wanted to shove him under the broken train or kick him until he was as motionless as his engine. But the fool went on and on with his breathless pleas.

"The fireman and I jumped out just in time, but look at the mess they made!"

Vidal eyed the blown-up rails, the blown-up train. Broken. Out of order. That's what the bastards in the woods wanted. Chaos. He stopped in front of a car that seemed somewhat intact.

"What did they steal?" he asked one of the men overseeing the transport.

"Nothing, Capitán. They didn't open a single car." The man wiped soot from his face. He was much calmer than the engineer. He was delivering good news.

"What the hell are you talking about?"

"This whole mess . . . They didn't open any of the wagons. They took nothing. God only knows what they wanted. Other than to waste our time."

Vidal watched his soldiers swarming around the broken train like ants around their trampled anthill. *Waste our time.* The words rang awfully false in his mind. No. The rebels wouldn't make use of valuable explosives just to annoy him. Or would they? The answer rang through the woods before he could finish his thought.

Another explosion made them all spin around. Another fireball was rising from the trees and there was no doubt about the direction from where it came.

Fooled! It had all been a ruse, a distraction!

But now this was war.

The fighting was still going on when they reached the mill—explosions tearing the soldiers' jeeps, trucks, and tents apart, blood-soaked bodies sprawled all over the yard. Vidal barely recognized Garces emerging from the smoke, covered in blood and soot.

"They came out of nowhere, Capitán!"

Vidal pushed him aside.

It was pouring, as if the sky were teaming up with the rebel beasts. Yes, that's what he would call them from now on. Beasts from the woods. The rain mixed with the smoke and made it hard to see where the attacks were coming from, but Vidal didn't remove his sunglasses. Their own reflections in the dark lenses—that was all he wanted his men to see until he'd regained control over his emotions. His mask was slipping and the eyes were the first to betray the rage and fear hidden behind it.

They'd been tricked like a bunch of rabbits by a fox, his equipment, his men, all reduced to a mess of rain-soaked trash. Vidal could hear the forest laughing at him, the forest and the cowards hiding under its trees.

"They have grenades, Capitán!" Garces's eyes were wide with fear. "There was nothing we could do." The soldiers all knew their *capitán* would find someone to blame and to bleed for this.

Only now did Vidal notice that the barn doors stood wide open.

He nearly crushed the sunglasses when he took them off with his gloved hand. Garces didn't dare follow him into the barn. The provisions, the medicine . . . the rebels had taken everything, even his tobacco. The doors, though, were still intact. No trace of explosives. Vidal inspected the lock. No sign of forced entry.

"Capitán!" Serrano ran to his side. His face couldn't hide his relief that Garces and not he had been in charge of guarding the mill this morning. "We've surrounded a small unit. They've taken cover up the hill."

The hill. Good. That would make the beasts into weak rabbits. Vidal straightened the cap on his wet hair. Yes. This time he wouldn't let them get away.

*

It was not much of a hill they had run to. The few rocks on top were the only cover the rebels had.

Vidal led the attack himself, shooting as he ran from tree to tree. This time he would kill them before the forest could hide them again. As always, when he went into battle, he was holding the watch in his left hand. It was his good-luck charm, its broken face pressing against his palm, its ticking urging him forward. Sometimes it sounded like a metallic whisper: *Come on, Vidal. I saw the death of your father. I want to see yours. How long will you keep me waiting?*

He'd ordered his soldiers to attack the rebels' position from all sides. Bark splintered around them in the cross fire, but he knew their foes would soon run out of ammunition. There were probably a dozen of them, maybe fewer. They were hopelessly outnumbered.

The hunt didn't taste as good as it usually did. Vidal had allowed himself to be fooled by the prey. No revenge would erase that shame. But at least he could make sure no one would live to tell the story. He hid behind a tree to reload his pistol. Serrano took cover behind a tree to his left.

"Go ahead, Serrano!" Vidal yelled, stepping out to take another few shots. "No need to be afraid, this is the only decent way to die!"

He took cover again and inhaled deeply as he slipped the watch into his pocket. It still protected him. Obviously, his time to die hadn't come yet. Another few shots, bullets missing him by an inch, while his soldiers screamed around him and fell on their backs to stare with empty eyes up into the branches and the pitiless rain. Back behind another tree to push fresh bullets into the pistol, and out once more through the metal rain, up the hill, chasing prey out from behind the rocks, making them regret that they'd dared to make a fool of him.

Vidal took cover one last time. Rain dripped from the peak of his cap into his eyes. Corpses were sprawling their limbs over the rocks like pale roots torn out of the ground. Only two rebels were still fighting, but when Vidal ordered another attack they fell with muffled cries, hit by several bullets.

Oh, the silence of Death. There was nothing quite like it. Vidal often wished he could record it and listen to it while shaving his face. Its silence was only disturbed by the sound of the rain pouring through the trees and falling onto the lifeless bodies, soaking their clothes until they seemed to melt into the ground.

Vidal walked up the last stretch of the hill, followed by the soldiers who'd survived the attack. Their losses were nothing compared to the rebels. The first one Vidal stopped at didn't stir. He made sure he was dead nevertheless by firing twice into his silent face. It felt good. Each shot neutralized some of the poison the shame of being fooled had left in his blood. But he needed to find one who could still talk.

Serrano came, as always, running like a well-trained dog when Vidal called him to his side. They found another two of their enemies lying between the rocks on top of the hill. They were only boys, maybe fifteen years old. One was dead, but the second one was still moving. He was pressing his right hand against a bullet wound in his neck, his pistol beside him. Vidal kicked it away.

"Let me see," he said, pulling the boy's bloody hand away from the wound. He said it almost gently. Vidal enjoyed being calm with his prey.

The boy still had some fight in him, but it was an easy task to pull his hand off the wound. He had no strength left and for sure not much life. The throat was covered with blood.

"Can you talk?"

The boy gasped for air, staring up at the clouds that were covering his face with rain.

"Damn it." Vidal got up and drew his pistol.

When he pointed it at the boy's head, the fool reached up with his blood-stained hand to push the muzzle aside, his fading eyes filled with defiance, almost mockery. Vidal yanked the pistol out of his grasp and took aim again. This time the boy pressed his hand against the muzzle, but the bullet went easily through flesh and bone. Vidal put another bullet into his rebellious head.

"These are useless. Neither of them can talk." Vidal waved at the bodies covering the ground around them. "Shoot them all."

Serrano had watched the assassination of the boy uneasily. Vidal suspected Serrano sometimes imagined his own head beneath his *capitán*'s pistol. Garces for sure didn't have such thoughts. He went to work as ordered.

"Capitán!" he called. "This one is alive. Just a wounded leg."

Vidal stepped to his side. One look at the injured rebel was enough to make him smile.

"Yes, this one will do."

24

BAD NEWS, GOOD NEWS

Soldiers are usually silent after lost battles. Vidal's men, though, were shouting and laughing when they returned from the forest. Mercedes knew something terrible must have happened. The other maids were standing in the kitchen doorway watching the turmoil in the yard when she came running into the kitchen.

"What happened?" She was so breathless from fear she could barely speak. When had she last breathed calmly? She couldn't remember.

"They caught one. They caught one alive." Rosa's voice was shrill with panic. Rumors were she had a nephew in the woods. "They're taking him to the barn!"

They all knew what that meant.

Mariana called to Mercedes when she ran back out into the pouring rain, but Mercedes couldn't make herself be cautious. Not today. The fear she felt was a beast devouring her heart.

"Mercedes! Come back!" Mariana's voice was hoarse. The other maids gathered around the cook like a flock of frightened hens, their faces stiff with both fear and hope: fear that Vidal's men would drag Mercedes into the barn; hope that she might find out who they'd caught.

Who had they caught?

"Pedro!"

Mercedes whispered her brother's name as her feet slipped in the mud.

"Pedro!"

She'd almost reached the barn when she saw the soldiers dragging their prisoner in through the open door, his legs helplessly ploughing the muddy ground behind him. Mercedes took another step to glance into the barn, but all she could see were the soldiers, their rain capes shimmering in the dark, tying a limp figure to one of the wooden beams inside.

"Mercedes?"

Vidal was standing behind her with Serrano at his side.

"Capitán." She was surprised the sound her lips formed made any sense. She could barely take her gaze off the prisoner. His head was hanging down, his face hidden under a dark cap. Her brother wore a cap like that.

"I need . . . to check on the supplies in the barn."

Surely he heard how desperate she was. Even to her own ears she sounded

153

like a lost little girl. Luckily Vidal was far too eager to get to his prisoner to pay any attention.

"Not now, Mercedes," he replied impatiently. "I want no one in the yard or the barn. Check on my wife, if you'd be so kind. . . ."

She nodded obediently. But she couldn't move. She just stood there and watched Vidal take the cap off the prisoner's drooping head. He raised his face and looked at her.

Tarta.

His eyes were as wide as those of a lamb being dragged into the slaughterhouse. Wide with the knowledge of what was about to come. Mercedes felt his gaze like a hand reaching for hers, but Tarta didn't give her away. He didn't scream for help, he pressed his lips together, determined to be brave, those lips that broke words like porous clay.

Mercedes was still standing in the rain when Serrano shut the barn doors. She was ashamed to feel relief that they'd caught Tarta and not Pedro. The relief only lasted for a moment, though. Tarta knew where Pedro was. And he knew all about her and the doctor.

He knew everything.

Mercedes was surprised her feet found the way back to the kitchen. The others were chopping vegetables for the soup they would serve the murderers. *Is my brother still alive?* she kept asking herself as she joined them to cut roots and parsley. And how about the others? Were they all dead in the woods, their blood mixing with the rain? *No!* She told herself. *No, Mercedes, they wouldn't have kept Tarta alive if they'd killed them all.*

154

Slowly, as if her fingers belonged to someone else, she cut another root into pale slices with her apron knife. All she saw was the knife's sharp blade. What was happening in the barn? It took all her strength to prevent her thoughts from going back to the wide-eyed boy and imagining what they would do to him.

Mariana was watching her, her round face lined by life. "That's plenty, dear," she said when Mercedes pushed the chopped vegetables over the table and reached for another root. Which line was life drawing right now onto their faces? So many lines, of fear, of grief . . . Mercedes was surprised she was still beautiful.

Mariana held up a tray of food she'd prepared for Ofelia and her mother. "Shall I take this upstairs?" Mariana didn't have loved ones in the woods, but she had two sons of almost the same age as Tarta.

"I'll do it," Mercedes said, taking the tray from her hands—anything to prevent her imagination from running wild, but it didn't work. *What has happened to Pedro?* The question repeated itself at every step she took up the stairs. *What is Tarta telling them?*

Dr. Ferreira was with Ofelia's mother. He looked up from the glass of medicine he was preparing when Mercedes walked in. *Do you remember Tarta?* she wanted to ask him. *How he can't read the newspaper fast enough for the others? Now he can give us all away if they make him talk.*

Ofelia didn't notice Mercedes's fear.

She was too happy to notice. Her mother felt well enough today to play cards and when Dr Ferreira handed her the glass with medicine she shook her head.

"I don't think I need it, Doctor," she said. " I feel so much better."

"That's why I'm giving you only half the dose, and yes, you're much better," Dr. Ferreira replied with a smile. "I don't understand why, but I'm glad."

Ofelia knew. She looked at the jug of fresh milk Mercedes had brought. The mandrake would soon need it. Along with a few drops of blood. All would be well even though she'd disobeyed the Faun and caused the death of his Fairies. She still heard their screams in her dreams, but her mother was smiling again and, after all, she had fulfilled the second task and brought back the Pale Man's dagger.

Yes, the Faun would understand.

In her heart Ofelia knew that he wouldn't, but she was too happy to allow those worries to cast a shadow.

25

TARTA

Vidal was taking his time. To question a prisoner was a complex process. It resembled a dance, one slow step back, then a fast one forward, and back again. Slow, fast, slow.

His prisoner was shaking and his face was streaked with sweat, though they had only roughed him up a little. His fear was doing most of the work so far, the fear of what was going to come. It would be easy to break him.

"Damn, this cigarette is good. Real tobacco. Hard to find." Vidal held the cigarette so close to the boy's face he felt the heat of the burning tobacco.

Tarta tilted his head back when his captor pressed the cigarette to his trembling lips.

157

"G-g-go to hell."

"Can you believe it, Garces?" Vidal turned to his officer. "We catch one and he turns out to be a stutterer. We'll be here all night."

"As long as it takes," Garces replied.

Tarta could tell this officer didn't enjoy the situation as much as his *capitán*, who was the kind of uniform-wearing devil Tarta had always dreaded meeting. He was in their hands and he knew what those hands would do. *If you're ever caught, think of someone you need to protect*, Pedro had taught him, when they'd practiced how to stay silent even under torture. *Someone for whom you'd die. It may not help, but it doesn't matter. Think of some-one, Tarta.* Who? Maybe his mother. Yes. Though thinking of her might make it worse as he could just imagine how she would cry if she lost him.

Tarta lowered his head. If only his limbs would stop shaking. Even if Pedro's advice could help his mind escape, his body betrayed his fear.

"Garces is right," the *capitán* said. "As long as it takes."

He opened his shirt, the cigarette dangling from his lips. Tarta wondered whether he'd take it off to not ruin it with his blood. "You'd do better to tell us everything. But to make sure you do, I brought along a few tools. Just things you pick up along the way."

Vidal picked up a hammer. He had lined up his tools very orderly on an old wooden table.

Shaking. Didn't people say one could die from fear? Tarta wished he knew how to make his fear kill himself.

"At first I won't be able to trust you." The Devil weighed the hammer in his hand. He was clearly proud of his torturing skills. "But after I use this, you'll own up to a few things. Once we get to these—" He picked up a pair of pliers. "We'll have developed . . . how can I put this . . . ?"

Tarta detected a hint of discomfort, maybe even compassion on the other officer's face. He had the same mustache as Tarta's father.

"Let's say it this way." The Devil opened and closed the pliers. "We'll have grown much closer by then . . . like . . . brothers. And when we get to this one—" He held up a screwdriver. "I'll believe anything you tell me."

Tarta started sobbing. He tried so hard not to, but there was so much fear in him, so much loneliness and despair. It all had to take some kind of shape, even if it was just tears.

His captor took another satisfied puff from his cigarette and put the screwdriver back on the table. Then he picked up the hammer again and approached Tarta.

"I'll make you a deal," he said, pressing the hammer's heavy head against Tarta's trembling shoulder. "If you can count to three without stuttering, you can go."

Tarta lifted his head to look at his torturer even though he knew his eyes would give away how desperately his terrorized heart wished for a glimmer of hope. He also looked for it in Garces's face . . . Garces, yes, that was his name. Tarta was glad the rebels didn't tell each other their true names; he was too good at remembering them.

Garces's mustached face was drained of any expression.

"Don't look at him!" the Devil snapped. "Look at me. Above me there's no one. Garces?"

"Yes, Capitán."

"If I say the asshole can leave, would anybody contradict me?"

"No one, Capitán. If you say so, he can leave." Garces returned the shaking boy's glance. *That's all I can do for you*, his eyes seemed to say. That I don't look away.

Vidal took another puff from his cigarette. Oh, he enjoyed this so much.

"There you have it." He brought his face once again close to Tarta's. "Come on. Count to three."

Tarta's trembling lips tried to form the first number, while his body cringed in fear.

". . . One."

"Good!"

Tarta stared at the ground, as if he could find some last shreds of dignity there. His lips tried again, and then he pushed the syllable out.

". . . Two."

Vidal smiled. "Good! One more and you're free."

Tarta's mouth twitched with the effort to speak clearly—trying to deliver unbroken words to the man who would break him. But this time Tarta's tongue wouldn't obey. All it uttered was a stuttered "T-t," the tremor of a broken thing.

He looked up at the Devil, his eyes pleading for mercy.

"Shame," Vidal said, summoning a note of compassion to crown his performance.

Then he drove the hammer down into the pleading face.

THE BOOKBINDER

Once upon a time, there was a bookbinder called Aldus Caraméz, who was such a master of his craft that the queen of the Underground Kingdom entrusted him to bind all the books for her famous crystal library. Caraméz's whole life was contained in those volumes, as he had been very young—still a boy—when the queen asked him to bind the first book for her, which was a volume that contained drawings by her mother.

The bookbinder still remembered how his hands had trembled as he spread the delicate portraits of fairies, ogres, and dwarves on his workbench; of toads (whom the queen mother had a special affection for), dragonflies, and of moths nesting in the tree roots that covered the ceilings of the palace like curtains of breathing lace. For the binding, Caraméz had chosen the skin of an eyeless lizard, whose scales reflected candlelight almost as lushly as silver. These lizards were fierce creatures, but the king's hunters slayed one from time to time when they tried to prey on the queen's peacocks, and Caraméz always claimed their skin for his craft, imagining he'd give them eyes by making them into books—quite a naive idea, but he liked it.

The queen loved the first book he had bound for her so much that she kept it on her bedside table, along with a volume Caraméz had bound for her daughter, Moanna, just a few weeks before she disappeared. Caraméz had created a whole library for the lost princess, and it held hundreds of the most richly illustrated books about the animals of the Underground Kingdom, its fabulous creatures and often miraculous plants, its vast underground land-scapes, and all its different peoples and rulers.

Moanna had just turned seven—oh yes, Caraméz remembered those days very well—when she requested a book about the Upper Kingdom. "What tales do they tell their children up there, Aldus?" she had asked. "What does the moon look like? Someone told me it hangs like a huge lantern in the sky. What about the sun? Is it true it's a huge fireball swimming in an ocean of blue skies? And the stars . . . do they really resemble fireflies?"

Caraméz remembered the sharp pain that had pierced his heart when the young princess had asked those questions. Many years before, his older brother had asked these same questions and a year later, he had disappeared, never to come back. When the bookbinder shared his concerns with the queen, she replied: "Create and bind her the book she asks for, Caraméz. Make sure it contains everything she wants to know, for that way she won't try to see the moon and the sun with her own eyes."

But the king didn't agree with his wife. He forbade Caraméz to fulfill his daughter's wish, and the queen decided to not fight his decision, as she had to admit that her daughter's request troubled her as well.

Princess Moanna, though, kept asking her questions.

"Who told you about the Upper Kingdom, my princess?" Caraméz asked when she once again visited his workshop, requesting that he at least make her a small book about the birds of the Upper Kingdom. Moanna had never seen a bird. Bats were the only flying creatures in the Underground Kingdom. And fairies.

The princess answered Caraméz's question by handing him a book. Of course! Her parents' library! Libraries don't keep secrets; they reveal them. The book Moanna handed the bookbinder contained reports from her mother's ancestors who had traveled extensively in the Upper Kingdom.

"Keep it," Moanna said, when Caraméz hid the book hastily behind his back. "I don't need the book. I'll just listen to the roots of the trees. They know everything about the Upper Kingdom!"

It was the last time the bookbinder talked to the princess before she disappeared. Caraméz still remembered her voice, though there were days when he couldn't recall her face. From time to time he still caught himself making a book for Moanna filled with tales the fairies told him or with stories whispering in the skins of the eyeless lizards.

Maybe the Faun had heard about those books. He usually didn't come to Caraméz's workshop. The Faun didn't believe in books. He was much older than the oldest manuscripts in the queen's library and could rightfully claim that he knew so much more about the world than all their yellowed pages. But one day he suddenly stood in the door of the bookbinder's workshop. Caraméz was slightly afraid of the Faun. He was never sure whether he could trust those pale blue eyes. In fact, he wouldn't have been surprised to learn that Fauns eat bookbinders.

"I need you to bind a book for me, Caraméz," the Faun said softly. His voice could be as soft as velvet or as sharp as a lizard's fangs.

"What kind of book, my horned lord?" Caraméz asked with a respectful bow.

"A book that contains everything I know but will only show what I tell it to reveal."

Caraméz frowned. He was not sure he liked the idea of such a book.

"This book will help Princess Moanna find her way back," the Faun added.

Of course. He knew how fond Caraméz was of the lost princess. The Faun knew everything.

"I will do my best," the bookbinder replied.

The Faun nodded his horned head, as if that was all he asked for, and handed him a bundle of pages.

Caraméz eyed them with surprise.

"But these pages are empty!" he said.

"No, they aren't," the Faun replied with a mysterious smile. "This paper was made from the clothes Princess Moanna left behind, and the added glue contains all the knowledge I have of the Upper Kingdom."

He reached up with his clawed fingers and plucked a roll of brown leather out of the thin air.

"This leather," he said, "was cut from the skin of a beast that fed on truth and many fearless men. I want you to use it for the cover of the book. That way the leather will give the princess courage whenever she touches it."

Caraméz unrolled the leather on his workbench and rubbed the empty pages between his fingers. Both materials were of the very best quality. They would make a beautiful book, even though the paper still looked empty to him.

"Go to work immediately," the Faun ordered. "I just learned I may need the book very soon."

Caraméz obeyed. He went to work straightaway. But he added one ingredient he didn't tell the Faun about: he mixed a few of his tears into the glue for the binding, for he was sure the princess would need not just courage and knowledge to guide her way back, but also love.

ONLY TWO GRAPES

This time Ofelia was awakened by laughter, a soft, hoarse laughter echoing in the darkness that drowned her room like black milk.

"I see your mother is much better, Your Highness." The Faun looked enormously pleased with himself. "Surely you must be relieved!"

He looked even younger now, though his goat legs still creaked with every step he took toward Ofelia's bed. Despite the ancient patterns covering his cheeks and forehead, his skin was so smooth it reflected the light of the almost full moon.

"Yes, thank you," Ofelia replied, casting a nervous glance at the Faun's satchel peeking out from under her blanket. "Things haven't turned out that well, though. Not all of them, I mean."

"Ah? No?" The blue cat eyes widened in surprise.

Ofelia was sure he already knew. She'd come to believe the Faun knew everything—about this world and any other.

"I . . . had an accident," she murmured, handing him the satchel. The surviving Fairy was chattering inside. Ofelia hadn't dared to let her out, fearing she might come to harm as well.

"An *accident*?" The Faun repeated the word in unveiled disbelief.

He opened the satchel and growled.

The Fairy fluttered out and landed on his shoulder. The longer the Faun listened to her, the more sinister his face became until he finally bared his pointed teeth and groaned with anger.

"You broke the rules!" he roared, pointing a claw at Ofelia.

"It was only two grapes!" she cried, hastily pulling the red velvet-wrapped dagger from under her pillow. "I thought no one would notice!"

The Faun snatched the dagger, and shook his head in anger. "We've made a mistake!"

"A mistake?" Ofelia could barely hear her own voice.

"You have failed!" snarled the Faun, towering over her. "You can never return!"

Ofelia felt as if the night were opening its mouth and swallowing her.

"But it was an accident!"

"No!" the Faun roared again, his eyes narrow with rage and contempt. "You—can—not—return! Ever!" Each word hit Ofelia like a stone. "The

moon will be full in three days! Your spirit shall forever remain among the humans."

He bent toward her until his face nearly touched Ofelia's.

"You shall age like them. You shall die like them! And all memory of you—" He stepped back, his hand raised as if to enforce the prophecy. "You shall fade in time. As for us"—he pointed accusingly at the Fairy and at his own chest—"we will vanish with you. You will never see us again!"

Then his body melted into the night, as if Ofelia's disobedience had turned him and the Fairy into mere shadows dissolved by the light of the waxing moon. And Ofelia sat in her bed, filling the silence they left behind with desperate sobs.

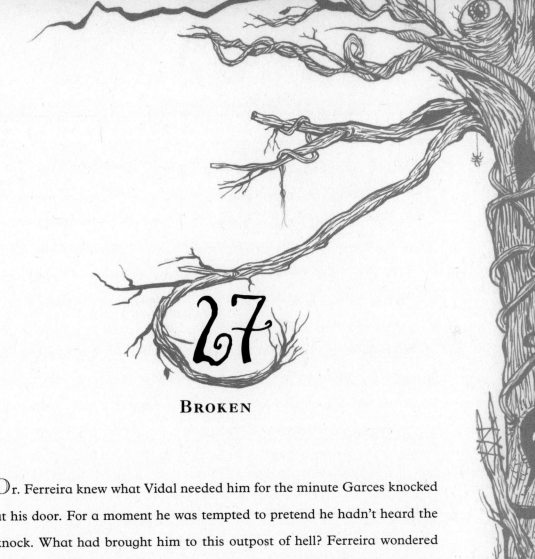

27

BROKEN

Dr. Ferreira knew what Vidal needed him for the minute Garces knocked at his door. For a moment he was tempted to pretend he hadn't heard the knock. What had brought him to this outpost of hell? Ferreira wondered while following Garces into the rain: fate or his own decisions? It had rained all night, and the day promised to continue under a weeping sky.

Appropriate.

Vidal was standing in front of the barn, washing his hands in a bowl of water. Ferreira was not surprised to see the blood on his fingers. Yes, it would be exactly what he had expected. Another broken man.

"Good day, Doctor." Vidal was once again all virile pose. It was at times hard to not laugh at it, but Vidal was far too frightening a man to consider such a slip.

"Sorry to wake you so early," he said, rolling down his sleeves. "But I think we need your help."

His shirt was clean. Vidal always made sure of that. Appearance is vastly important for those who rarely take off their masks, and Ferreira had never seen Vidal without his. What had he looked like as a child? Had his gaze been already as emotionless as now? Had he ever called someone his friend? The mask wouldn't tell.

While following Garces through the rain, Ferreira had tried to prepare himself by imagining what they'd done to the prisoner. His imagination had failed him. He almost didn't recognize the boy who had tried to read the newspaper in the cave in the woods.

Ferreira could barely keep his hands from shaking as he opened his bag. He felt so much rage, sadness, and helpless disgust as he pulled out bandages and disinfectant to clean the wounds Vidal's tools had inflicted. The boy was sitting on the floor, his back against the beam they'd tied him to, cradling his hand, if one could still call it a hand. Blood was running from his mouth, and one of his eyes was so swollen Ferreira wasn't sure it was still there.

Tarta . . . yes, that was the nickname the others had called him. He moaned when Ferreira gently took his arm to have a look at the shattered hand. The fingers were crushed, all of them. One was just a bloody stump.

"My god, what have you done to him?" The words just wouldn't stay in his mouth, although Ferreira knew it was unwise to comment like this. But what he saw made even wisdom nothing but a folly, a useless distraction from the cruelty of men.

"What we have done to him? Not much." There was a clear hint of pride in Vidal's voice. "But things are getting better."

Vidal had walked over to Ferreira's bag and pulled out a vial just like the ones he'd found up by the rebel campfire. Ferreira didn't notice. All he saw was the swollen face of the boy, the one open eye clouded with fear and pain, watching him.

"I like having you handy, Doctor," Vidal said behind him. "It has its advantages."

Ferreira was too busy to hear the hint of mockery. Four of Tarta's ribs were broken, probably kicked in. He heard Vidal order Garces to come back to the house with him.

Good! Leave! Ferreira thought, when they left him alone with the broken boy. *Before I call you what you are. If I find a name for it.*

"I talked," Tarta murmured. "Not much. B-b-but I talked."

The boy's visible eye asked for forgiveness. It tore Ferreira's heart into shreds like a piece of worn cloth. So much darkness. Too much of it.

"I'm sorry, son," he whispered. "I am so sorry."

The lips covered in blood tried once again to form words. The torture hadn't made it easier for them, but finally the letters came together.

"Kill me!" the boy begged. "Kill me now. Please."

Too much.

28

MAGIC DOESN'T EXIST

Vidal had kept the vials he'd found by the campfire in the woods in a drawer of his table. When he came up to his room to compare them to the vial he had taken from Dr. Ferreira's bag he wasn't surprised that they proved identical.

"Son of a bitch!" he hissed under his breath.

He had let himself be fooled by the softness of the good doctor's face. Another mistake. But he would fix this one.

Ferreira was still with Tarta when Vidal put the vials back into the drawer of his table.

The doctor was kneeling next to the tortured boy, unaware that his betrayal had been discovered. The liquid he'd pulled up in a syringe was as golden as the key Ofelia had taken from the Toad. Tarta had closed his eye, the one Vidal had left intact, but his mouth was open. Each breath was an act of courage, as it brought so much pain, and when Ferreira hesitated to place the needle, Tarta grabbed his arm with his one good hand to make sure the syringe found his flesh. He lifted his head for a last glance, a wordless thank-you from a boy whose life had been cursed by a tongue that wouldn't obey him. In the end it had made him a traitor of the only friends he had ever known.

"You'll see, this will take away the pain." Talking to the boy as if he was a normal patient brought Ferreira at least some peace. Tarta's eyes were closed again and blood was trickling onto his face from under his black hair.

"Yes, it's almost over," the doctor said softly.

He said it to himself. Death had already thrown her cloak of mercy over Tarta's shoulders.

Vidal didn't understand men like Ferreira. He had no doubt that a man who helped the rebels would of course also kill his unborn child.

Ofelia was under her mother's bed checking on the mandrake when Vidal came rushing up the stairs to make sure his son was still alive. His hasty steps filled the mill with the echo of his fear but Ofelia didn't hear them. She was too worried about the mandrake. The root wasn't moving anymore even though she'd given it fresh milk and another few drops of blood.

"Are you sick?"

She leaned over the bowl, when she suddenly felt hands grabbing her legs. Gloved hands. The Wolf pulled her brutally by the ankles and Ofelia found herself helplessly sliding out from under the bed.

"What were you doing down there?" He yanked her up and shook her so roughly Ofelia tasted hatred like a poisonous brew in her mouth.

Of course, he found the bowl. He sniffed at the milk and cringed in disgust.

"What the hell is this?"

Ofelia just shook her head. He wouldn't understand.

She cried out when he grabbed the mandrake out of the bowl and tried to free it from his grasp, but he held it out of her reach, milk running down his arm, while his other hand wouldn't let go of Ofelia.

Her cries woke her mother.

"What are you doing? Ernesto, leave her," her mother said weakly, pushing her blankets back. "Leave her alone, please!"

The Wolf thrust the dripping mandrake toward her face.

"Look at this thing!" Milk splattered Carmen's nightgown as he pushed the root into her hands. "What do you think of this? Heh? She was hiding it under your bed!"

Ofelia couldn't bear to look at her mother's face. It was pale with disgust.

"Ofelia?!" she said, her eyes begging for an explanation. "What was that thing doing under my bed?"

The Wolf walked to the door, his steps stiff with anger.

"It is a magic root!" Ofelia sobbed. "The Faun gave it to me."

"This is all because of that junk you let her read." The Wolf was standing in the doorway, but Ofelia could still feel the sting of his fingers around her arm.

"Please leave us! I'll talk to her, *mi amor*!"

Ofelia hated the tenderness in her mother's voice and her eagerness to please a man who barely looked at her.

Children do notice those things, for all they can do is to watch—and hide from the storms the adults create. The storms and the winters.

"As you wish," Vidal said, reminding himself there were more important matters to deal with than a lonely widow who'd spoiled her daughter. Things would change once his son was born.

Ofelia was shaking when he finally left her alone with her mother. So much rage, first the Faun's and now the Wolf's. She couldn't say who frightened her more.

"He told me you would get better!" she cried. "And you did!"

"Ofelia!" Her mother dropped the mandrake on the bed and caressed her face. "You have to listen to your father! You have to stop all this!"

Father. Oh, it was so hard to not hate her for calling him that—and for being too weak to protect her. Ofelia threw her arms around her and pressed her face into her shoulder. Her mother's nightgown smelled like the place they used to call home, where she had felt safe and happy.

177

"Please, take me away from here!" she begged. "Let's just go, please! Please!" But those were the wrong words.

Her mother freed herself from her embrace.

"Things are not that simple, Ofelia." There was no tenderness in her voice now. It was sharp with impatience. "You're getting older. You'll soon see that life isn't like your fairy tales."

She grabbed the mandrake and walked to the fireplace, each step painfully slow. "The world is a cruel place, Ofelia. And you need to learn that. Even if it hurts."

Then she threw the mandrake into the fire.

"No!" Ofelia tried to reach for the twisting root, but her mother grabbed her by the shoulders.

"Ofelia! Magic doesn't exist!" Her voice was hoarse with exhaustion and anger for all her dreams that hadn't come true. "Not for you, me, or anyone else!"

A shrill squeal rose from the fire. It was the mandrake—burning, writhing with pain, screaming like a newborn child as the flames were eating its pale limbs.

Carmen faced the fire and, for a moment, Ofelia could've sworn her mother could see the magic before her eyes—could hear the screams, could see the root writhe . . .

But then she gasped and grabbed the footboard. Her legs gave way and she slipped to the floor, her eyes wide with disbelief and panic, while the mandrake continued to squeal in the flames.

Blood. Blood was pouring from between Carmen's legs, staining her skin, her nightgown, the floor.

"Mamá!" Ofelia fell to her knees by her side.

"Help!" she cried. "Help!"

Down in the kitchen the maids dropped their knives. They all had been worried about Ofelia's mother and her unborn child. The doctor would help. They read the same thought on each other's faces.

But Dr. Ferreira was in the barn, kneeling by a dead boy, an empty syringe in his hand.

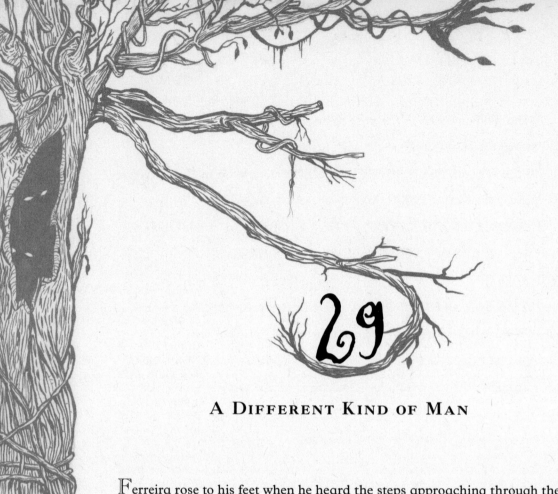

A Different Kind of Man

Ferreira rose to his feet when he heard the steps approaching through the rain. Garces was the first one to walk into the barn, lean, thick-skinned Garces, who could keep the pain of others at a comforting distance from his own heart. He stared at the tortured boy whose disfigured face was calm and at peace in death, while the other soldiers gathered in front of the barn doors, holding off the pouring rain with their umbrellas, so strangely tame a device in contrast to their uniforms.

Vidal was the last one to arrive. He knelt at Tarta's side to examine the dead body while Dr. Ferreira was putting the syringe back into his bag, closing it with the calmness of a man who had done his duty.

"Why did you do it?" Vidal rose to his feet.

"It was the only thing I could do."

"What do you mean?" There was a hint of surprise in Vidal's voice. Surprise, curiosity . . . "You could have obeyed me!"

He walked toward Ferreira as slowly as a predator stalking his prey, and stopped right in front of him. It was not easy to stand and just look up at him. But there are many kinds of courage. Ferreira had feared this man for so long—witnessed his butchery, healed the wounds he inflicted—he felt relieved he wouldn't have to pretend anymore to be on his side.

"Yes, that is true, I could have obeyed you," he said calmly. "But I didn't."

Vidal scrutinized Ferreira like a strange animal he'd never seen before.

"It would have been better for you. You know it. Why didn't you obey me?"

There was almost a hint of fear in his voice and in the way he pressed his narrow lips together. In his kingdom of darkness everyone gave in to fear, why not this soft spectacled man who barely dared to speak up in his presence?

"To obey . . ." Ferreira chose his words carefully. ". . . just like that, for the sake of obeying, without questioning . . . that's something only people like you can do, Capitán."

He turned to pick up his bag, then stepped out into the rain. Of course, he knew what was going to happen, but why not take the moment, the moment of being finally free of fear? He felt the cold rain on his face as he walked away from the barn. Such precious steps, so free, so at peace with himself.

He cast a glance over his shoulder, just when Vidal came out of the barn, with the long-determined stride of the hunter. Ferreira didn't turn or stop when Vidal drew his pistol. He kept on walking. When the bullet hit him in the back, he took off his glasses and rubbed his eyes, though he knew the fog filling them was the breath of Death. Two more steps. Then his legs gave way and there was only the mud and the fading rain. Ferreira could hear himself breathing. He was cold. Very cold. No memory came to him, no soothing words. For some inexplicable reason the only thing he noticed was a spider hidden between the stones of a wall a few feet away. The little animal appeared to his eyes, like a miracle: He could see every joint, every follicle, and every chitinous bump. The spider's architecture, its grace, its beauty, and its hunger all seemed to blend into a single thing: the last thing alive. Ferreira inhaled and drank muddy water. He tried to cough it out, but mid-cough his heart stopped.

One clean shot.

Vidal approached the outstretched body and crushed the glasses next to it under his boot. He still didn't understand why the fool hadn't obeyed him, but he was strangely relieved the good doctor was dead and he would never have to look into those soft and far-too-thoughtful eyes again.

"Capitán!"

Two of the maids were standing in front of the barn, their faces pale with worry. Vidal pushed the pistol back into his holster. He could barely make sense of what they were saying. His wife was not well, that's what he finally picked up from their frightened nattering—and that his son was on the way, while the doctor who had been supposed to help with his birth was lying dead in the mud behind him.

182

When the Faun Fell in Love

There is a forest in Galicia so ancient some of the trees remember a time when animals took the shape of men and men grew wings and fur. Some men, the trees whisper, even became oak and beech and laurel and drove their roots so deeply into the ground they forgot their names. There is one fig tree especially whose story the others like to tell when the wind makes their leaves murmur. It grows on a hill at the heart of the forest. One can spot it easily, as the two main branches bend like the horns of a goat and the trunk is split, as if the tree gave birth to something growing under its bark.

Yes! the forest whispers. *That's why the trunk is split open like a wound. This tree did give birth, for it was once a woman who danced and sang under my canopy. She picked my berries and braided her hair with my flowers. But one day she met a Faun who liked to play his flute under my trees in the moonlight. He'd fashioned the flute from the finger bones of an ogre and his tune sang of the dark underground kingdom he came from, so different from the light the woman carried inside.*

All this is true, and she fell in love with the Faun nevertheless, with a love as deep and inescapable as a well, and the Faun loved her back. When he finally asked her to come with him to his underground world, however, she dreaded the thought of spending the rest of her life without ever seeing the stars or feeling the wind on her skin. So she decided to stay and watched him leave. However, the love she felt filled her with such longing, her feet grew roots to follow her beloved underground, while her arms reached for the sky and the stars she'd chosen over him.

Oh, the heartache she felt. It made her soft skin turn to bark. Her sighs became the rustling of the wind in a thousand leaves and, when the Faun came back one moonlit night to play his flute for her, all he found was a tree whispering the name he had never told anyone but her.

The Faun sat down between the tree's roots and felt his own tears like dew on his face. The branches he sat under showered him with flowers, but his lover couldn't throw her arms around him or kiss his lips anymore. He felt such a pain in his wild and fearless heart that when he caressed the tree his own skin—once covered with silken fur—became as rough and wooden as the bark of his lost love.

The Faun sat under the tree all night until the sun rose and drove him away. Its bright light had never become him and when he had returned to the dark womb of the earth, the tree bent her branches deeper and deeper in sadness until they resembled her lover's horned head.

Eight months later, on a full moon night, the trunk of the tree split with a soft moan and a child stepped out. It was a boy, graced with the beauty of his mother, while the horns in his green hair and the hooves on his slender legs gave away his father. He pranced and danced down the hill like his mother had once danced under the trees, and he made himself a flute from bird bones to fill the forest with a song that sang of love and loss.

Deep underground, where he was instructing a princess in the tasks of her parents' court, the Faun heard the flute's music. He excused himself and rushed through secret passageways known only to him to the Upper Kingdom. But when he arrived, the sound of the flute was nowhere to be heard, and all he found was a track of small hooves on the wet moss, washed away by the rain after a few dancing steps.

30

DON'T HURT HER

Her mother was screaming. Ofelia was sitting on a bench a maid had put outside her mother's bedroom and she could hear it through the wall. The Wolf was sitting next to her, just an arm's length away, staring blindly at the wooden railing through which she had sometimes watched the maids in the hall below. Did he also, Ofelia wondered, feel the urge to throw himself over the handrail each time her mother let out another tormented scream? To shatter the aching heart on the stone tiles just to find relief from all the fear and pain? But life is even stronger than Death, so Ofelia stayed on the bench next to the Wolf who had lured her mother to this house to scream and bleed.

Ofelia was sure everything would have been all right if her mother hadn't thrown the mandrake into the fire. Or if Ofelia had only hidden it better. And if she'd resisted the grapes of the Pale Man. . . .

Another scream.

Did she wish her brother to die for hurting her mother so badly? She couldn't say. She wasn't sure of anything anymore. Her heart was so numb from all that fear and pain. Did her brother make their mother scream because he was as cruel as his father? No. He probably couldn't help it. After all, no one had asked him whether he wished to be born. Maybe he'd been happy where he was before. Maybe it was the same world the Faun claimed she came from. In that case she'd have to tell her brother how hard it would be to get back to it.

One of the maids rushed by with a jug of water.

Vidal followed her with his eyes.

His son. He would lose his son. He didn't care about the woman scream-ing in that room. A tailor's wife . . . wrong choices throughout all his life. He should have known she was too weak to keep his son safe. He needed that son.

In the bedroom behind him Mercedes was fighting Death. Along with the medic and the other maids.

Everything was red with blood: the sheets of the bed, the hands of the medic who was used to the screams of injured soldiers but not to the pain life caused coming into this world and the white nightgown Ofelia's father had sown for Carmen.

Mercedes turned away from the bed.

Blood . . . it seemed to be everywhere. She had heard by this time about Ferreira lying in the mud, his blood mixing with the rain, and about Tarta, whose blood was dyeing the straw on the barn floor. Mercedes went to close the bedroom door even though she knew the girl sitting outside could hear the screams through the wall. How she pitied her. The child's pain hurt her more than the mother's.

Another scream.

Ofelia felt it like a knife cutting a slice off her heart. Another maid rushed out into the corridor holding heaps of blood-soaked linen. And then . . . the screams and moans weakened . . . faded . . . and stopped.

A terrible silence seeped through the wall and filled the corridor.

Then the shrill voice of a crying baby pierced it.

The medic stepped out of the room, his apron and hands covered with blood. The Wolf got up.

"Your wife is dead."

The medic lowered his voice, but Ofelia heard him.

The world was as hard and comfortless as the bench she was sitting on, as barren as the whitewashed walls around her. She felt her tears like cold rain on her face. She hadn't understood until now what it meant to be alone, utterly and completely alone.

Ofelia somehow managed to rise to her feet and slowly walked over the wooden floorboards, worn smooth from the steps of long-ago people, toward her mother's room where the baby was crying. His screams sounded like the squeals of the mandrake. They did. Maybe magic existed after all. For a moment Ofelia even thought that her brother was calling her name, but then she saw the empty face of her mother. Her opaque eyes, dull as an old mirror.

No, there was no magic in the world.

⁓

They buried Carmen the next day, right behind the mill. It was a colorless morning and as she stood by the grave Ofelia felt as if she'd never had a mother. Or that maybe she had just walked away into the forest. Ofelia couldn't imagine her in that plain coffin, so hastily built from a few planks of wood by a carpenter the Wolf had summoned from one of the nearby villages.

The priest was a small old man. He looked as if Death would get him next.

"Because the essence of His forgiveness lies in his words and in His mystery . . ."
Ofelia heard the words, but they didn't make sense. She was alone, all alone, though Mercedes was standing behind her and she now had a brother. The Wolf held him in his arms. To give him a son . . . that was all her mother had been needed for.

The priest kept on talking, and Ofelia stared at the hole the soldiers had dug in the muddy ground. Maybe this had always been what she and her mother'd come to the mill for: to find this grave, to meet once again with Death. There was no place one could escape her. Death ruled everywhere. When had her mother known, Ofelia wondered, she would never leave this place?

"Because God sends us a message, it is our task to decipher it."

The priest's words sounded as much a judgment as the words the Faun had yelled at her in his rage. Yes, her mother had been judged as well. Ofelia couldn't get rid of that thought as she watched her brother sleeping in his father's arms. She didn't want to look at them. They had killed her mother.

"The grave takes in only a hollow and senseless shell. Far away now is the soul in its eternal glory . . ."

Ofelia didn't want her mother's soul to be far away. But when she went back to her mother's bedroom, she couldn't find her there. Far, far away . . .

Some of her fairy-tale books were still on the bedside table as if nothing had changed—and as if she still had a mother.

Because it is in pain . . . the priest's voice whispered in her head . . . *that we find the meaning of life and the state of grace that we lose when we are born.* The bottle with the drops Dr. Ferreira had given her mother to help her sleep was on the bedside table. Ofelia held it up to the window, letting the amber liquid catch what little morning light there was.

God in His infinite wisdom puts the solution in our hands.

Ofelia put the bottle into the suitcase Mercedes had already packed with her mother's few clothes, and picked up her books. There was another suitcase on the table where her mother would have her tea, and underneath the window stood the wheelchair.

Because it is only in His physical absence that the place He occupies in our souls is reaffirmed.

While Ofelia was staring at the empty chair, two ravens flew past the window, so beautiful, so free. Where had her mother gone? Was she with her father now? Would he forgive her that she'd died giving birth to another man's child?

Ofelia turned her back to the window.

No. There was no God. There was no magic.

There was only Death.

31

The Cat and the Mouse

The night had come, wrapping the last remains of the day in black funeral clothes. Mercedes was in Vidal's room, holding his baby, the motherless baby, wishing the boy to be fatherless too, wishing him to never meet the man who was leaning over his table, unharmed and unmoved by his wife's death. Mercedes had never known her own father, but looking at this one she considered herself lucky. What kind of man would his son become growing up in such darkness?

She gently put the boy back into the cradle and covered him with a blanket. His father was holding one of the phonograph records he played all day and well into the night. Mercedes heard the music even in her dreams by

194

now. His hands were so gentle with the records that one could almost make oneself believe he'd used a different pair of hands to break Tarta's bones and shoot the doctor in the back. She missed Ferreira. He had been the only one at the mill whom she could trust.

"You knew Dr. Ferreira pretty well, didn't you, Mercedes?"

Vidal wiped the record with the sleeve of his uniform, the uniform she'd scrubbed for hours to get the blood out.

Don't show any fear, Mercedes.

"We all knew him, *señor*. Everyone around here."

He just looked at her. Oh, how well she knew his games by now. *Don't show any fear, Mercedes.*

"The stutterer spoke of an informer," he said as casually as if they were discussing what to eat for dinner. "Here . . . at the mill. Can you imagine?" His arm brushed hers as he walked past her. "Right under my nose."

Mercedes stared at her feet. She couldn't feel them. Fear made them numb. Vidal put the record on the phonograph.

Don't look at him. He'll see—he'll know!

Panic constricted her throat and as hard as she tried to swallow, her fear was like a rope strangling her. Behind her the baby began to softly complain, almost muffled, as if he didn't yet know how to cry.

"Mercedes, please." Vidal waved her to the chair in front of his table.

It was so hard to make her feet move, although she knew any glimpse of hesitation would betray her. Maybe it was too late anyway. Maybe Tarta had given them all away. Poor, broken Tarta.

"What must you think of me?" Vidal filled a glass with brandy he kept in his bottom drawer. The tomcat was playing with the mouse; Mercedes had known him far too long to have any illusions about the outcome of this game. Fear filled her throat with broken glass as she sat down sideways, so she didn't have to face Vidal. And to keep the illusion that she could jump up and run.

"You must think I'm a monster." He held out the glass to her.

Yes! she wanted to scream. *Yes! For that's what you are.* But her lips managed to say words he would hopefully want to hear:

"It doesn't matter what someone like me thinks, *señor.*"

She took the glass almost hastily, hoping he wouldn't notice her shaking hand. He filled another glass for himself and gulped the brandy. Mercedes still hadn't touched hers. How could she drink with the glass in her throat? *He knows. . . .*

"I want you to bring me some more liquor. From the barn." He pushed the cork into the bottle. "Please."

"Yes, *señor.*" Mercedes put her untouched glass on the table. "Good night, *señor.*"

She got up.

"Mercedes . . ."

Poor mouse. The cat always gives it that moment of hope.

"Aren't you forgetting something?"

"*Señor?*" She turned around slowly, a fly caught in amber, the tree's sap hardening around her.

196

He opened the top drawer of his table.

"The key." He held it up. "I do have the only copy, don't I?"

Terror stiffened her neck, but she managed to nod. "Yes, *señor*."

He got up from his chair, weighing the key in his hand as he walked around the table.

"You know, there's an odd detail that's been bothering me. Maybe it's not important but—" He stopped right in front of her. "The day the rebels broke into the barn with all those grenades and explosives . . . the lock itself wasn't forced."

Answering his glance took all her courage. All of it.

"As I said." His eyes were as black as the muzzle of the pistol he had shot Ferreira with. "It's probably not important."

He clasped his fingers around hers when he handed her the key, his fingers that had broken Tarta's with a hammer.

"Be very careful."

The tomcat clearly didn't want the game to end yet. Why else would he warn her? Yes. He wanted to watch her run and shoot her in the back like Ferreira. Or chase her like a deer after he stirred her out of the thicket she was hiding in.

Vidal loosened his grip, his eyes still on her.

"Good night, *señor*." She turned once again, surprised her legs were obeying her. *Walk, Mercedes!*

Vidal watched her leave. All tomcats enjoy letting the mice go. For a while. After they felt their claws.

He walked over to the phonograph and dropped the needle onto the record. One could have danced to the music. Appropriate, as he'd just initiated another deadly waltz and this time the prey was especially beautiful.

Vidal approached the cradle and looked down at his son.

The woman who had given birth to him had been beautiful too, but Mercedes was stronger. Which meant it would be so much more enjoyable to break her, much more enjoyable for sure than to torture that stutterer or to shoot that noble idiot of a doctor. And he had a son now. Someone to teach what life was about.

He would teach him its cruel dance. Step by step.

32

IT'S NOTHING

Though Mercedes yearned to run, she walked down the stairs, worried her shaking knees would make her stumble. The *capitán* didn't follow her, not yet, but there wouldn't be much more time.

She pushed aside the tile in the kitchen floor and took out the latest batch of letters she'd been entrusted to deliver to the men in the woods, letters from mothers, fathers, sisters, lovers. A woman's voice drifted down from Vidal's room singing softly of love and its torment, as if he were teasing her with his music, each note the tip of a knife pressed against her throat.

He knows.

Yes, he did, and she would end up like Ferreira with her face in the mud—though Vidal would probably prefer her to die on her back like Ofelia's mother, while giving him another son. For a moment Mercedes just stood in the dark kitchen, held by the song drifting down from above, as if his fingers were still grabbing her hand, those murderous bloodstained fingers.

Go, Mercedes. He can't tie you down with a song. No. But she couldn't leave the girl. Not without saying goodbye.

Ofelia was fast asleep, although the night was still young, when Mercedes slipped into the attic room, the night of her mother's funeral. Grief exhausts the heart. Vidal's music drowned the treacherous creak of the door and the sound of Mercedes's steps as she approached the bed. Most times it seemed as if the old mill was on the soldiers' side, but sometimes Mercedes found the old house to be a friend.

"Ofelia! Ofelia, wake up!"

Mercedes grabbed the girl's shoulder without taking her eyes off the door. "Ofelia!" *Please wake, please. . . .*

The girl's eyelids, heavy with sleep, finally opened. Mercedes bent over her, grabbing her hand.

"I am leaving, Ofelia."

The eyes opened wide, such beautiful eyes, as beautiful as her mother's, but beauty was a dangerous gift in this world.

"Where are you going?"

"I can't tell you. I can't."

Mercedes cast another gaze at the door. The music was still seeping in, as if Vidal was weaving his web into the night.

"Take me with you!" Ofelia grabbed her arm. "Please!"

"No, no!" Mercedes whispered, caressing the frightened face. "I can't!"

The girl threw her arms around Mercedes's neck. She was too young to be alone in the world, far too young.

Mercedes kissed her hair, as raven-black as her own, and held her in her arms the way she'd once wished to hold a daughter of her own. "I can't, my child! I will come back for you, I promise."

But Ofelia wouldn't let go. She held on so tightly Mercedes could feel her heartbeat.

"Take me with you!" she begged. "Take me with you!" Over and over again.

How could anyone say no in the face of such loneliness?

Stumbling through the night, they followed the brook, shuddering under another pour of freezing rain. The old umbrella Mercedes had grabbed barely sheltered them from it. One time she believed she heard Ferreira's footsteps behind her and had to remind herself that he was dead, like Tarta and so many others. *Dead.* Did the word become more or less real with every time one had to attach it to a loved one?

"Wait!" Mercedes stopped, her arm firmly around Ofelia's shoulders.

She thought she could hear a horse snorting, but when she listened keenly into the night, all she could hear was the rain drumming against the trees and dripping from the leaves above them.

201

"It's nothing!" she whispered, pressing Ofelia to her side. "Don't worry. Let's go."

But the game was over.

As Mercedes turned, lifting the umbrella, she gazed into Vidal's face. Garces stood behind him and at least twenty more of his soldiers. How had she not heard them? The night is always on the hunters' side.

"Mercedes." Vidal turned her name into a chain around her neck. He let his gaze wander across her face, so stiff with terror, and down to the girl.

"Ofelia."

He didn't try to veil his hatred.

He grabbed the girl's arm and left Mercedes to Garces.

They will kill her. That was all Ofelia could think, while the Wolf dragged her back to the mill, through the forest, over the mud-covered yard, into the house, where her mother had died. *They will kill Mercedes like they killed my mother.*

The Wolf pulled her up the stairs with hands of iron. He called for one of his soldiers to guard the door before he pushed her roughly into her room.

"How long have you known about her?"

He slapped Ofelia's face. It was still wet with rain, or was it tears she felt on her cheeks? It didn't matter. The raindrops were tears too. The whole world was crying.

"How long have you been laughing at me, little witch?!"

The Wolf shook her and Ofelia felt his wish to do more. Break her. Slash

202

her like one of the rabbits the cook prepared in the kitchen for him and his men. Finally, he let go of her with a rude curse and took off his cap, breathing heavily, smoothing his hair. For the first time there was a crack in his mask and it frightened Ofelia more than the Faun's rage. The Wolf would never forgive that she'd seen him weak—just as he wouldn't forgive that she hadn't told him about Mercedes.

"Watch her!" he barked at the soldier by the door. "And if anyone tries to get in"—he put the cap back on his head, straightening it, closing the crack—"kill her first."

Ofelia's cheek stung as if the slap had split her skin. She started crying the moment the Wolf closed the door, all those tears: for her mother, for Mercedes, for herself.

33

JUST A WOMAN

And there she was, tied to the beam stained with Tarta's blood while outside a new day was breaking. Mercedes didn't look at Garces as he tightened the ropes and bound her hands in front of her, the same way they had tied Tarta's.

Vidal was busy searching her bag. He had taken off his gloves. He often did when he questioned a prisoner. It was so hard to clean the blood off the leather. Mercedes knew. She'd done it quite a few times.

"Chorizo . . ." He threw the sausage on the ground. "That was not supposed to feed just you and the girl, right? And for sure you didn't steal this for the girl." He sniffed at a small parcel. "My best tobacco. You should

204

have asked for it. I would have given it to you, Mercedes."

Garces smiled and tied another knot, while his *capitán* pawed through the letters she was to deliver to the men in the forest.

"I want the names of whoever wrote these. I want them by tomorrow." He handed the letters to Garces.

"Yes, Capitán."

Why hadn't she left the letters behind? All the loved ones the soldiers would now come for . . . Nothing would hurt the men in the woods more. All those words of love would turn into weapons against the ones they were supposed to comfort.

Mercedes tried to fight back the tears. Despair welled up like poisoned water in her heart. Love is such a terribly efficient trap, and the cruelest truth about war is that it makes loving a deadly risk. *We'll kill your mother. We'll rape your sister. We'll break your brother's bones.* . . .

Mercedes leaned her head back against the splintered wood. What did it matter if they killed her now? She'd been afraid of this for far too long. Her heart was so exhausted from all the fear that it felt nothing except regret about the letters and compassion for the people who'd soon hear a knock at their doors.

Vidal unbuttoned the shirt she had washed and ironed for him. How often had she cursed the stains the blood of someone else had caused? Would hers stain the sleeves or would he take the shirt off? Yes, think about washing shirts, Mercedes. Don't give your mind time to think about what he'll do to you.

"You can go, Garces."

She wasn't sure what she sensed in the look Garces gave her. Some of the soldiers didn't like to torture women. His *capitán* didn't have any such hesitations. She suspected he enjoyed it even more than breaking men.

"You're sure, Capitán?"

Mercedes couldn't remember having ever heard Vidal laugh before. "For God's sake! She's just a woman."

Mercedes stared at the wooden walls of the barn. That would be the last thing she'd see. The dead flanks of trees, while the living forest outside was out of reach. Garces closed the barn doors behind him.

"That's what you always thought. That's why I was able to get away with it. I was invisible to you."

Mercedes continued staring at the wall so her captor wouldn't see the fear in her eyes. But Vidal stepped to her side and grabbed her chin, forcing her to look up at him.

"Damn. You found my weakness. Pride." He examined her face like it was a piece of beautiful meat. All his to make it bleed. "Luckily it's my only one."

Liar. Mercedes felt his fingers pressing into her cheeks. How he enjoyed her helplessness, how he enjoyed making her beauty into something he could own by destroying it.

"And now let's find out about *your* weakness."

Vidal let go of her face and strode to the table that held his tools.

"It's very simple," he said, turning his back to her as he picked up the

206

hammer. "You will of course talk . . ." He laid the hammer back on the table, surveying the other tools as if not sure which one to use. "But I have to know that everything you say"—he picked up an iron hook, scrutinizing it tenderly—"is the truth."

Keep talking, Mercedes prayed as her fingers searched silently for the knife hidden in her apron. Would it be sharp enough? Sharp enough to cut rope instead of carrots and onions?

"Yes, you will talk. We have a few things here strictly for that purpose." He still had his back turned to her.

Mercedes was sure Tarta had heard the same speech. Vidal liked to boast. After all, a *capitán* stationed at an abandoned mill in the middle of a Galician forest didn't have much to boast about except his cruelty. Pride? No, vanity—*that* was his weakness: the urge to constantly prove to himself and to others that nothing and no one could withstand him and that his heart didn't know either fear nor pity. Liar. He was afraid of everything. Especially himself.

Mercedes kept her eyes on his back as she cut the fibers of the rope.

"We use nothing special . . . it's not necessary. One learns about these things on the job."

Oh yes, he liked to hear his own voice. He was proud of the fact he could keep it calm even when his heart was beating fast with rage or excitement. Mercedes was sure it was beating faster at the prospect of using that hammer on the face he'd gazed upon so often, on the hands he'd touched so casually whenever she came close. Invisible. Yes. Mercedes, sister of

Pedro and of another sister who'd died far too young, daughter of parents long dead . . . her true Self had been invisible to him. But Vidal had always noticed the beauty of her body.

There. She felt her knife's blade against her skin. Her hands were free. But there was more to cut.

"At first . . ." Vidal held up a pair of pliers. "Yes, I think this one will do." He still hadn't turned.

Mercedes silently loosened the rope from around her legs. Her feet sank deeply into the straw as she tiptoed toward her captor.

She thrust the knife through the white shirt into his back. She used all the strength she had left, but the slim blade was short, and muscles and flesh are not as easy to cut as the fibers of a rope. Vidal moaned and grabbed at the wound, while Mercedes stumbled back, trying to catch her breath. She'd never driven a knife into human flesh and her weapon felt as fragile as her body.

How wide his eyes were with disbelief, when he finally turned to face her. Just a woman. This time Mercedes plunged the knife into his chest. He collapsed as she yanked it out, but she'd caught him underneath the shoulder, far too high for his heart—if he had one—and the blade was just too short. Mercedes thrust it one more time, although her fingers were already slippery with his blood. This time the knife went between his opened lips and Mercedes pressed the blade against the corner of his mouth.

"You see? I'm not some old man, *hijo de puta*," she hissed at him.

"Nor a wounded prisoner."

She slashed the knife up into his cheek. Then she peered down at him, on his knees, pressing his hand against his bleeding mouth.

"Don't you dare touch the girl." She barely recognized her own voice. "You won't be the first pig I've gutted."

Her knees spoke another language. All her fear seemed to have gathered in them, but she made it to the barn door and pulled it open. Mercedes didn't even notice that she still had the bloody knife in her hand when she stepped outside. She managed to hide the blade once again in her apron and she began to walk. Past the soldiers in the yard. None of them paid attention to her.

Invisible.

Only one turned his head. An officer. Serrano. He stared after her, but Mercedes kept walking. A radio was blaring in front of the stables, announcing the winning numbers of the lottery the cook always spent her money on.

Keep walking.

"Hey, did you see that?" Serrano called over to Garces, who was frowning in disappointment at the rebels' lottery ticket he'd kept after picking it up in the woods. "Can you believe it?"

Serrano's face was blank with bewilderment. "He let her go."

He pointed at Mercedes. Garces crumpled the lottery ticket in his hand and threw it to the ground. "What are you talking about?"

Mercedes walked faster. She felt Garces's eyes on her back. Maybe he didn't enjoy torture as much as his *capitán* but he for sure didn't mind killing.

"Hey!" he called after her. "You! Stop!"

Mercedes began to run.

Oh, this was easy.

Garces pulled the pistol out of his holster.

So much easier than taking a hammer to a tied-up prisoner.

He took aim as carefully as Ofelia's father had put yarn through the eye of a needle.

"Get her, Garces!"

But Garces had forgotten about Mercedes. He lowered his pistol and stared at his *capitán* stumbling out of the barn like a drunk, his shirt covered in blood, his hand pressed over his mouth.

"Come on!" It was hard to understand what Vidal was saying with his hand over his mouth. "Bring her to me!"

Garces didn't move. He just stared at the blood seeping through Vidal's fingers. "Capitán, what . . ."

"Bring her to me, damn it!"

This time the hand came down. The mouth that yelled at Garces opened wide into Vidal's left cheek. It wasn't easy to take one's eyes off that bloody grin, but Garces finally managed to lower his gaze.

"Mount up!" he shouted to his soldiers.

Mercedes had just reached the trees when she heard Garces bark his order. *Why didn't you kill him when you had the chance?* she asked herself when she looked back and saw Vidal. If she'd had a better knife she would have done it. Yes, she would. She stumbled on through the wet ferns, their fronds brushing her skin and her clothes. Mercedes hadn't run like this since she was a little girl, and then it had been for the joy of running.

Joy. How did that feel? She couldn't remember. . . .

She soon had to lean against a tree to catch her breath, even though she heard horses snorting behind her, their hooves trampling down the ferns, their riders yelling. So many of them and she kept stumbling over roots and rocks while they came closer and closer.

A clearing opened between the trees. Tall pines standing in a wide circle as if they had gathered to watch her die. The soldiers encircled Mercedes with their horses when she had barely crossed half of the clearing. Her hair had come loose and she felt as small and vulnerable as a child.

Garces smiled down at her, his gaze mocking and admiring her at the same time. All women were prey. *Look at her*, Garces's eyes said. *Quite beautiful for a maid.* He calmed his horse, caressing its neck as if it was hers. He took his time getting out of the saddle. He was enjoying this. The fun was just starting.

"Shhh," he said, walking toward her, holding his hands up soothingly as if he were calming a child.

Mercedes had always believed Garces to be less cruel than Vidal, but what did that matter? He was one of them. She reached for her knife. Its blade was still red with his *capitán*'s blood when she pointed it at him.

Garces took off his uniform cap, still smiling as if he was courting her.

211

"You are going to stab *me*? With that little knife?"

Oh, how she wished to be a man.

"It'll be better if you come with us without struggling. The *capitán* says if you behave . . ." How a man's voice could turn into a cat's purr when he was hunting a woman.

Mercedes pressed the blade against her throat. Tarta hadn't had that chance. Poor Tarta.

"Don't be a fool, sweetheart." Garces took another step toward her.

Mercedes pressed the knife so firmly against her throat she felt the blade prick her skin. Garces kept walking.

"If anyone's going to kill you," he purred, "I'd rather it be me."

He was still smiling at her when he died.

The bullet hit him in the back. The others tried to flee, but they fell one by one. while Mercedes was still pressing the knife to her throat. Her ears were numbed by the shots and the screams when she finally lowered it. Around her, panicked horses were slipping in the grass, dropping their riders at her feet, and the clearing was covered with the bodies of dying men.

Mercedes couldn't tell if any of the soldiers managed to escape. If yes, it wasn't many. She only saw a few horses galloping into the forest, wild and free for the first time in their lives. And there was Pedro. When her brother came walking toward her, followed by his men, it felt as if he were emerging from a dream, a good dream for a change. He pulled her into his arms and Mercedes cried, holding him tight, weeping at his shoulder, weeping, weeping, while his men shot at the soldiers still stirring among the trampled ferns.

Shots and sobs . . . the sounds of the world. There had to be more than that, but Mercedes had forgotten. She hugged Pedro and it seemed as if she'd never stop crying.

The Tailor Who Bargained with Death

In A Coruña there once lived a young tailor named Mateo Hilodoro, who was happily married to Carmen Cardoso, a woman he had loved since childhood. He felt like the richest man on earth when she gave birth to their daughter, who he loved as much as his wife. They called the girl Ofelia. Mateo sewed all her clothes himself and made dresses for her dolls, copying the robes the princesses wore in his daughter's fairy-tale books.

Mateo Hilodoro was indeed a very happy man. But on the night of Ofelia's birthday his hand cast the shadow of a skull onto the green linen he was cutting to tailor a new dress for her. Hilodoro stepped back from his workbench to find Death standing behind him. Her face was as white as her dress.

"Mateo," she said. "Your time is up. The queen of the Underground Kingdom needs a tailor, and she chooses you."

"Tell her I am no good!" he pleaded. "Tell her my hands shake and my seams dissolve after just a few days!"

Death shook her head, though her pale face betrayed a trace of compassion.

"Your stitches are more perfect than a nightingale's song, Mateo," she said. "And there can be no such perfection in this world."

"If you take me I'll cut off my fingers!" the tailor exclaimed. "And what use will I be to her then?"

"You won't need this body where I'll take you," Death said. "All you need is your craft—and you can't cut that out of you, for it is your very essence. An immortal spark, you might say."

Hilodoro hung his head and cursed the gift he'd believed to be a blessing all his life. His tears dropped onto the fabric he had been cutting for his daughter's new dress. Ofelia would have looked so beautiful in it, with her mother's dark hair and her wide and thoughtful, ever-questioning eyes.

"Just let me finish this dress!" he begged. "I promise once I've sewn the last stitch, I'll come with you willingly and I'll tailor the most beautiful clothes for the queen of the Underground Kingdom."

Death sighed. She was used to men begging for another few years or months, sometimes even hours. There was always something unfinished, something undone, unlived. Mortals don't understand life is not a book you close only after you read the last page. There is no last page in the Book of

Life, for the last one is always the first page of another story. But the tailor moved her. There was so much love in him . . . and kindness—a quality Death had found to be rare among men.

"So be it. Finish the dress," she said with a slight hint of impatience—mostly impatience with herself for giving in to his pleas. "I will be back."

Hilodoro's hands shook when he returned to his workbench, and his stitches were uneven. He had to undo them all as they mirrored his despair the way they had once mirrored his happiness. While he cut the thread and plucked it out of the delicate fabric, a bold thought caused him to lift his head.

What if he didn't finish the dress? What if he *never* finished the dress?

He began to stay up every night and wouldn't listen when Carmen asked him to get some sleep, for he wanted to make sure that Death believed he was working on the dress by day and by night. For every stitch he finished, he secretly undid another, so secretly that he hoped not even Death would catch him.

Six weeks later his hand once again cast a skull's shadow onto the green linen of the still-unfinished dress. Death was standing behind him, but this time she wore a red dress.

"Mateo!" she said, her voice cold as a grave. "Finish the dress before the sun rises or I will take the child you sew it for as well."

Hilodoro felt how the needle pierced his skin as he clenched it in his hand, and a drop of blood fell onto the sleeve he was sewing. His daughter, Ofelia, would wonder where that dark spot came from.

"I will finish it before the sun rises," he whispered. "I swear. But please don't touch my child. She is so young."

"I can't promise that," Death replied. "But I will make you another promise: if you finish this dress tonight, it will wrap her in your love. Whenever she wears it and as long as it fits her, I will not come for her."

34

ONE LAST CHANCE

Tap, tap, tap. . . . The guard was walking back and forth in front of Ofelia's door, back and forth, to keep himself awake. The round window, twin of the full moon by day, was blackened by the night, which would end all hope to fulfill the Faun's tasks. All was lost. She'd never find out whether he'd told the truth that there still was a place she could return to and call home.

A place where she still had a mother and a father.

Watch her. And if anyone tries to get in, kill her first.

"Kill her?" She'd been waiting for someone to do that since the Wolf left—sitting in her nightgown on the floor, under which the Pale Man

219

roamed, her back against the foot of the bed—waiting for someone to come in and slit her throat.

Ofelia had placed the suitcase with her mother's clothes beside her, hoping it might give her some comfort, but it only whispered: *She is gone. They are all gone: your mother, Mercedes, even the Faun has abandoned you.* It was the truth. All that was left was the old mill filled with ghosts and the terrible man who had been the death of her mother and would kill Mercedes, too. Yes, he would for sure kill her. Ofelia wondered only whether she was already dead or whether the Wolf would take his time with her, as they said he'd done with the rebel boy.

Through the steps of the soldier outside her door she heard her brother crying down in the Wolf's den. He sounded so lost and lonely. His crying mirrored the moaning of Ofelia's own heart and spun a bond through the night between them. Though she still blamed him for her mother's death.

Ofelia raised her head.

There was another sound—a rustling of wings shaped like withered leaves.

The Fairy was fluttering above her, a living reminder of her dead sisters and of Ofelia's failure. She landed on Ofelia's hand, grabbing one of her fingers. She weighed less than a bird and the touch of her delicate hands filled Ofelia's heart with light and warmth.

"I've decided to give you one more chance." The Faun appeared from the shadows, holding out his hands as if he were carrying a precious gift.

Ofelia scrambled to her feet.

"One last chance." The Faun's narrow lips wore a forgiving smile.

Ofelia threw her arms around him and pressed her face into his long pale-yellow hair. It felt like embracing a tree, and the Faun's laughter was a bubbling spring feeding joy to her desperate heart. He caressed her hair, leaning his patterned cheek against her head, and Ofelia felt safe despite the soldier in front of her door, despite the Wolf, despite the suitcase with her mother's empty clothes. The Faun's huge body shielded her from a world that had grown so dark. Maybe she could trust him after all. Who else would help her? There was no one.

"Yes, I give you one more chance," the Faun whispered into her ear. "But do you promise this time to do everything I say?"

He took a step back, his hands still on her shoulders, and looked at her inquiringly.

Ofelia nodded. Of course. Everything! She would do everything she could just to have him protect her from the Wolf who'd dragged her back to this room like a rabbit caught in the woods.

"Everything?" The Faun bent down until he could look straight into her eyes. "Without question?"

He caressed her face with his clawed fingers and Ofelia nodded again, though this time she sensed the menace in his request.

"This IS your last chance." The Faun gave weight to every single word.

Ofelia remembered the grapes on the Pale Man's golden plates. No. This time she would be stronger. She nodded.

"Then listen to me." The Faun tipped his claw playfully against her nose. "Fetch your brother and bring him to the labyrinth as quickly as you can, Your Highness."

That was a task Ofelia hadn't expected.

"My brother?"

She couldn't help but frown. *What do you care?* she asked herself. *Yes, he sounds as lonely as you are, but he is his father's son and your mother would still be alive without him.* But not for the first time another voice inside her whispered, *He couldn't help it. He had to come to this world even though he was as scared of it as much as you are.*

"Yes," the Faun said. "We need him now."

For what? *Oh, Ofelia!* her mother used to say with a sigh. *Too many questions! Can't you for once just do what I say?* How, when her heart was asking them so persistently?

"But—" she began carefully.

The Faun's finger shot up, a withered warning. "No more questions. As we agreed, yes?"

Will you do everything I tell you? Everything. . . . Ofelia took a deep breath. The menace dwelled in that word, but she had no choice, did she?

"His door is locked."

The Wolf's room was always locked since he started keeping his son in there.

"In that case," the Faun said, smiling mischievously, "I'm sure you remember how to create your own door."

The chalk he produced out of thin air was as white as the piece he'd given her to enter the Pale Man's lair.

222

35

THE WOUNDED WOLF

Vidal was in front of his mirror rinsing his slashed face when he heard hoofbeats outside. Two of his soldiers had made it back from the forest, but no one dared tell the *capitán* the others were lying dead in a clearing among the trees, their blood dripping from fern fronds, while Mercedes, who had cut him like a pig, was alive and free.

Vidal inspected the grotesque grin Mercedes had given him. The kitchen knife had sliced his skin as efficiently as it sliced vegetables. When he tried to open his mouth, a jolt of pain made him shut his eyes, but he still saw Mercedes with the slim blade sticking out of her hand like the thorn of a wasp.

One of the maids had left the curved sewing needle he'd requested on his table. Mercedes had probably stitched his clothes with it. Vidal picked up the needle and shoved it through his lower lip. Each stitch made him wince, but he pulled the black thread through his flesh over and over again to get rid of the grin that made his own face mock him for what a fool he'd been.

Ofelia was listening to his moans through the door the Faun's chalk had opened in her floor. She could even see the Wolf standing in front of his mirror, and right underneath her a ladder was leaning idly against some boxes that were gathering dust in the back of the room. The Faun had made sure she could get to her brother's cradle easily. It was standing just a few steps away from it, and though Ofelia couldn't see him she could hear him softly crying. Maybe he was calling for his mother. Their mother . . . *Don't think about her, Ofelia! Remember where you are!*

She slipped into her shoes and drew her dark woolen coat over her nightgown.

The Wolf didn't seem to hear her as she climbed down the ladder. He was still standing in front of his mirror, with his back to her, groaning with pain. There was blood on his shirt. Ofelia didn't know who had wounded him, but she was grateful to whoever had dared to attack him, though she could feel his anger. As soon as she stepped from the ladder onto the floor she hastily slipped under the Wolf's table to hide from his gaze in case he turned around.

But Vidal still didn't turn.

He was scrutinizing the work the needle and thread had done. They had erased the grin Mercedes's kitchen knife had drawn. All the mirror showed was a thin bloodstained line, embroidered with black yarn, running from the left side of his mouth up his cheek. He covered it with a bandage and inspected his face one last time. Then he walked over to his table.

Ofelia dared not breathe. She could have touched his legs when he poured himself a glass of brandy. Her brother let out a feeble squeal in his cradle and the Wolf groaned when the sharp liquor seeped through his bandage. Ofelia heard him pour himself another glass and . . . set it down on the table.

Ofelia felt her feet and hands go cold with fear.

The chalk. Where was the Faun's chalk?

It was lying among Vidal's papers on the table. Vidal picked it up and crumbled it between his fingers as he scanned the room for the intruder who left it there.

Oh, how Ofelia feared her pounding heart would give her away!

And maybe Vidal did hear it.

He pulled out his pistol, walked around the table, and cast a glance underneath. But Ofelia had been fast. The Wolf saw nothing, and her brother came to her aid by starting to cry. Vidal holstered the pistol, and approached the cradle. His son . . . would he rule the boy's thoughts the way his father still ruled his? Would his son yearn to please him even with his death?

"Capitán! With your permission?"

He couldn't remember the name of the soldier who rushed into his room. They died too quickly.

"What?"

They all knew how severe the punishment could be for disturbing the *capitán* in his room.

"Serrano is back. He's wounded."

"Wounded?" Vidal was still scanning the room.

His son was crying as if something or someone were disturbing his sleep.

Please! Ofelia pleaded. *You will give me away, brother.* But the pile of empty burlap sacks she had slipped behind kept her safe from the Wolf's gaze, and finally she heard him walk toward the door.

Ofelia didn't leave her hiding place until she heard his steps on the stairs outside. He had left the half-empty glass of brandy on the table. It reminded Ofelia of other glasses—the ones Dr. Ferreira had prepared for her mother to help her sleep. She slipped her hand into her pocket. Yes, there it was. The bottle of medicine she had taken from her mother's room. She poured just a few drops into the liquor, afraid the Wolf would taste it if she added too much. Dr. Ferreira, her mother, her father, Mercedes . . . maybe they were all waiting for her in the Underground Kingdom the Faun had told her about.

All she had to do was do everything he said and she would see them all again.

Another squeal came from the cradle. Brother. Nobody had named him

226

yet. As if her mother had taken his true name to her grave. Ofelia remembered how she'd talked to him when he was still in her womb. She had warned him of this world. Yes, she had.

She bent over the cradle and took the baby into her arms. He was so small.

36

SISTER AND BROTHER

How they all stared at him when he walked into the dining room. Gone was the glory, the feeling of invincibility. They had last gathered to celebrate their victory in the woods. Vidal felt the bloody bandage on his cheek like a branding. Failure . . . slashed onto his face with a kitchen knife.

Serrano was sitting on a chair beside the fire, his heavy body deflated and slumped.

"Where's Garces?"

Serrano shook his head. Vidal sat down on the chair next to him.

"How many were there?"

"Fifty. At least. Only Garcia and I escaped. The rest didn't make it."

228

Serrano could barely look at him.

"Our watch posts aren't responding either," said the soldier who'd delivered the bad news to Vidal. He still couldn't remember his name. "How many men do we have left?"

"Twenty. Maybe fewer."

Vidal felt for the pocket watch, but he had left it on his table. He couldn't help but wonder whether it had announced his father's approaching death by ticking louder. He tried to mock the thought with a smile, but the pain this caused him was another reminder of just how badly things had gone wrong.

If he couldn't get his hands on Mercedes, he would kill the girl.

Ofelia was still standing in Vidal's room holding her brother. So small, so warm, his face all fresh and new under the white cap their mother had made for him, his eyes, clear and trusting, looking up at her.

Sister. Brother.

Ofelia had never been a sister before, just a daughter and a girl who'd ruined her new dress in the woods and still wasn't sure what the moon-shaped mark on her left shoulder meant.

Sister. The word changed everything.

"We're leaving," she whispered into her brother's ear. "Together. Don't be afraid."

Her brother uttered a timid whimper. *This is all new to me*, Ofelia believed to hear him say. *Please protect me, sister.*

"Nothing is going to happen to you." She pressed him firmly to her shoulder.

That is such a tough promise to keep.

She was walking toward the door when she heard his father's voice on the stairs. Oh, why hadn't she left a moment earlier?

"When the rest of the squad gets back, have them report to me immediately." The Wolf's voice was close. Too close.

Ofelia hid behind the door. *Don't cry, brother!* she begged silently. *Don't give us away!* Though he hadn't listened to her pleas for their mother's life.

"Radio for enforcements," she heard the Wolf say. "Now."

And there he was, back in the room. *Hold your breath, Ofelia.*

The Wolf walked over to his table and put the watch that lay next to the glass into his pocket. Then he reached for the liquor. Ofelia slipped out from behind the door the moment he turned his back and gulped the brandy down. Her brother slept peacefully in her arms and his trust in her made it easy to trust her luck. But it didn't hold. Ofelia had just made it through the open door when an explosion shook the walls of the mill. It came from the yard. The shine of flames ripped the cloak of the night and painted the walls around Ofelia in bright reds and whites. The Wolf spun around and saw her standing in the doorway, frozen like a hunted deer, with his son in her arms.

"Leave him!" His voice was a knife, a hammer, a bullet.

Ofelia held the Wolf's gaze and shook her head. That was all she managed to do.

The Wolf took a step toward her but he swayed, barely keeping his balance, and Ofelia sent a prayer of thanks to Dr. Ferreira for protecting her from his murderer.

Then she turned. And ran.

Vidal followed her, but he barely made it through the door. His head was swimming. What was wrong with him? He didn't suspect the brandy, he was too proud to consider the idea that a child had drugged him. No, it was the wounds the other witch had dealt him. He would find and kill her as well, but first the girl. He had known she would bring bad luck the moment she'd gotten out of that car. Her eyes were like the forest, her face so full of silence. He couldn't wait to break her neck.

She was still on the stairs when Vidal stumbled out of his room, but he was barely able to draw his pistol and the wretched girl was out the door before he could take aim. He saw her disappearing under the trees when he finally made it down the stairs and stepped outside. Why had she taken his son? Would she bring him to the rebels so they could kill him as revenge for her mother's death?

No. For the rebels had come to the mill. The trucks and tents were burning, there was smoke and fire everywhere and men fighting, their silhouettes as black as paper cuts against the red flames. Vidal should have killed the girl. And Mercedes. For she had kept her promise to Ofelia. She'd come back for her with her brother and his men. But when she and Pedro reached Ofelia's room, it was empty. Mercedes called Ofelia's name but there was no answer. All they found was her pale green jacket—and the outline of a door, drawn with white chalk on the floor.

THE ECHO OF MURDER

Once upon a time, a nobleman ordered five of his soldiers to arrest a woman named Rocio, who he accused of being a witch. He told them to drown her in the pond of a mill deep in the old forest where she lived. It required two men to drag her into the cold water and one to hold her down until she ceased to breathe. That soldier's name was Umberto Garces.

Garces had killed before, but his master had so far never ordered him to kill a woman. The task was terrible, and at the same time it aroused him, maybe because the witch was quite beautiful.

It usually didn't bother Garces to kill. He was surprised he couldn't find sleep that night.

He couldn't sleep for ten days, for the moment he lay down he once again felt the cold water on his skin and saw the witch's hair floating on the surface of the pond. When, on the eleventh night, those visions once again haunted him, Garces got up from his bed, saddled his horse, and rode through the moonlit forest back to the mill.

Garces had hoped it would give him peace to see the water of the pond unstirred and the witch's body gone from sight, as though she'd never existed. When he stepped closer to the water, though, Garces wished he'd never returned. The water was as black as his sin, and the trees seemed to whisper his judgment into the night: *murderer!*

Surely, she *had* been a witch. Wasn't this the proof? This could only be her doing! The whispering trees, the visions and sensations that haunted him . . . she had cursed him. They had been right to kill her. So right!

Garces felt the guilt lift from his heart, all that disgust with himself, the regret—gone. Maybe he should become one of those witch hunters who cleansed the country of them. The Church paid them very well and as he'd killed one already, he figured it would be easier the next time. Yes. He would be able to do it again. And again.

He laughed. And turned to walk back to his horse.

But he couldn't move.

The mud held his boots as firmly as if fingers had grabbed them.

Curse her! He was sure it was her.

"I'd do it again!" he shouted over the silent water. "You hear me?"

His boots sank deeper into the mud and his hands started to itch. He lifted them to his face. His skin was covered in warts and webs were growing between his fingers—the fingers he'd used to hold the witch down.

He screamed in terror so loudly the sound woke the miller and his wife. They didn't dare venture outside, though, to find out what all the noise was about.

Garces screamed again. By now his voice had changed. Hoarse croaking escaped his throat and, his spine twisted and bent until he fell to his knees, digging his webbed fingers into the mud.

Then he leaped into the same muddy pond water he'd drowned the witch in.

37

THE FINAL TASK

This time the Fairy didn't come to guide Ofelia. She had to find her own way through the labyrinth. The last task is always the hardest.

The explosions at the mill continued to tear through the silence of the night, but her brother was peaceful in her arms and part of that peace found its way into Ofelia's heart. She was sure the Wolf was following her, though she couldn't see him through the smoke drifting up from the mill. A wolf . . . No, he was not a wolf. Her fairy tales were wrong to give evil the shape of a magnificent wild creature. Both Ernesto Vidal and the Pale Man were human beings who fed on hearts and souls because they had lost their own.

The walls of the labyrinth welcomed Ofelia like a familiar embrace and soon the stone-framed circles it wove around her and her brother made her feel safe despite her pursuer. *He won't find you here,* she believed to hear the stones whisper. *We'll hide you from him.*

But Vidal was close behind, close enough to see the girl go through the arch and enter the labyrinth, though he was still stumbling from Ferreira's drops. Ofelia was fast and young, but she was carrying her brother, and the night air helped Vidal clear his fogged head. His finger twisted around the trigger of his pistol as he stumbled through the ancient corridors following the sound of Ofelia's footsteps like a hunting dog follows the scent of a deer. But each time he thought he was getting close, there was another corner, another turn, another wall . . . as if he himself had become the prey caught in an inescapable trap.

Where was she? Shaking his head to clear the fog away, he stumbled onward, one hand gripping the pistol, the other groping the withered walls. *Why had she come here, of all places?* He paused to catch his breath and listened for the girl's steps. There! So light, so fast . . . but her breathing was heavy by now. No wonder, she was carrying his son.

Ofelia could hear Vidal's steps behind her, but she was sure the opening with the well and the staircase was close, very close. Just around that corner. She turned—and found herself in front of a wall.

The wrong way! She'd gone the wrong way. Everything was lost.

But the labyrinth had waited for her for a very long time, and when Ofelia turned to stare helplessly up the corridor she'd come from, the

237

stones behind her began to shift. She peered over her shoulder and saw the wall that had been blocking her way was parting: tree roots, reaching into the widening gap like wooden claws, were clearing a path for her. The roots brushed Ofelia's arms and legs as she hastened through the crevice and there it was: the clearing she'd been searching for, at its center the well and the staircase leading down to the monolith where she'd first met the Faun.

The wall closed behind Ofelia and her brother the moment she'd passed through and when Vidal reached it all he found was solid stone. He looked around in disbelief, his shirt soaked in blood from the gaping wounds Mercedes's knife had made. Ofelia heard him cursing on the other side of the stone wall. She barely dared to draw breath, fearing the wall would open and let him pass, but the stones didn't move. His footsteps faded and all she sensed was her brother's heartbeat through the thin fabric of her nightgown and his warm breath at her shoulder.

Peace.

Love.

"Quickly, Your Majesty, give him to me."

Ofelia spun around.

The Faun was standing at the other side of the well, the moon outlining his silhouette with silver. Ofelia felt herself hesitating with every step as she walked over to him, past the flat stone wall surrounding the well. "The moon is high in the sky, Your Highness!"

Ofelia had never seen the Faun so cheerful.

"We can open the portal!" he exclaimed, pointing to the well.

In his other hand was the Pale Man's dagger.

"Why is that in your hand?" Ofelia felt as if the cold blade were touching her skin. The Faun uttered a soft purr.

"Ah, that . . ." He gently caressed the dagger. "Well . . ." His voice sounded both casual and apologetic. "The portal only opens if we offer the blood of an innocent. Just one drop of blood."

He tried to make the word *blood* sound small, waving its weight away with his hands. "A pinprick, that's all!" he added, pinching his palm playfully with the dagger's sharp point. "It is"—he drew a circle of completion into the night—"the final task."

Cold. Ofelia felt so cold.

"Now, then!" The Faun pointed to her brother, his fingers dancing as eagerly as a swarm of flies. "Let's hurry! The moon won't wait."

"No!" Ofelia took a step back and shook her head, pressing the baby so firmly to her chest that for a moment she was worried she'd wake him. But he stayed sleeping as calmly as if her arms were the safest place on earth.

The Faun bent forward, his cat eyes narrow with anger and menace. "You promised to obey me!" He bared his teeth with a threatening snarl. "Give me the boy! Give—me—the—boy!"

"No! My brother stays with me." Ofelia gave him the firmest gaze she could summon. It was the only thing she could do: hold the Faun back with her eyes, make him see she would not change her answer, even though everything in her was shaking.

The Faun gave another purr. This time, though, it sounded like surprise. He lowered the dagger and tilted his horned head to look at her. "You would give up your sacred rights for this brat you barely know?"

"Yes." The Faun's face blurred through the tears in her eyes. Had they just welled up or had they been there since her father died? She couldn't tell anymore. "Yes, I would," she murmured, pressing her cheek against her brother's tiny head, so warm under the white cap their mother had spent so many nights making for him.

"You would give your kingdom for him who has caused you such misery?" This time the Faun didn't sound angry at all. Each word seemed a proclamation telling the world about the strange decision a girl named Ofelia had made. "Such humiliation," he added, challenging her once more.

"Yes, I would," Ofelia repeated.

Yes, I would. . . . Those were the words Vidal heard when he finally staggered into the clearing. Maybe Ofelia's voice had shown him the way, or the Faun's angry speech. Or maybe the labyrinth had been built just for this purpose—to have them all play their part in a story written once upon a time and long ago.

Vidal couldn't see the Faun at all. Perhaps his own darkness made him blind to too many things. Perhaps he already believed in too much grown-up nonsense to have room to see anything else. It mattered little. What mattered was that he was a few steps away from the girl who appeared to be talking to herself.

"Yes, I would," Ofelia said again, her voice a broken sob. She stepped away from the dagger, away from the well, away from the Faun, unaware of the man standing just a few steps behind her.

"As you wish, Your Highness." The Faun spread his hands in defeat, his fingers painting her future into the night.

He was still dissolving into the shadows when Ofelia felt a hand grabbing her shoulder. The Wolf stood behind her, the bandage on his face a blood-soaked mark. He pulled her brother from her arms, peering at him, as if he needed to make sure she hadn't harmed him.

I protected him! Ofelia wanted to scream. *The Faun wanted his blood! Didn't you hear?* But when she turned around, the Faun was gone and she was once again alone. All alone, without her brother's warmth to comfort her.

"No!" she cried. "No!"

Her arms felt so empty and it was so terrible to see the child in his father's arms that for a moment she wished she'd given him to the Faun after all. But what did it matter? They were both monsters thirsting for the blood of others.

Vidal took a step back, the baby in his arms. He didn't make the effort to take aim.

He shot Ofelia in the chest without even lifting his hand.

Her blood spread on her nightgown like an opening flower as Vidal holstered his pistol and walked away with her brother.

Ofelia lifted her hand and watched the blood drip off her fingers. Her knees gave way and she fell by the side of the well, her hand pressed against the wound the bullet had torn, but there was too much blood to hold it back.

It painted red patterns on her nightgown and ran down her arm, stretched helplessly over the well. The air rising from its depth cooled her skin, while the blood kept dripping from her fingers, deep down into the womb of the earth.

None of her fairy tales had ever ended like this. Her mother had been right: there was no magic. And she hadn't been able to save her brother. All was lost. Her breath grew shallow. She shivered: the ground was so cold. . . .

38

HIS FATHER'S NAME

Vidal found his way back easily. The labyrinth didn't try to keep him in. He had done what had been foretold, but he was not supposed to meet his fate inside its endless circles. The world outside would take care of him.

They were waiting for him—Mercedes; her brother, Pedro; and the men from the forest. They were marking the end of Vidal's path with their bodies, standing side by side outside the labyrinth in a half circle that mirrored the stone arch. The moment had finally arrived—Vidal felt as if he'd lived it a thousand times in his dreams. The moment to prove he was his father's son and to show his own son what a man's life was all about.

Stepping out from under the arch, Vidal returned the rebels' hostile glances one by one, until his eyes found Mercedes. She didn't move as he walked toward her with his son. Pedro was standing by her side. Vidal never knew he'd fought both sister and brother. He held his son out to the woman who had cut—but not killed—him.

"My son." The world needed to hear it one more time. And the child had to live, for he would live through him, as his father had in him, with every breath he took.

Mercedes accepted the baby. Of course. She was a woman, she wouldn't harm a child, not even his.

Slowly—as had been the ritual of his life—Vidal took the watch from his pocket and cradled it in his hands. *This is it*, he thought. *The glorious ending.* He was ready to step over the edge. Despite his dead soldiers and the burning mill reddening the sky, he felt no fear.

The spirit of his father filled him. Made him whole.

Mercedes stepped back to her brother's side, the baby in her arms while Vidal stared at the watch's shattered face, its hands counting away his last moments as meticulously, as it had counted away all the years since his father's death. He could still hear the ticking, even after he closed his fingers around the silver.

Vidal cleared his throat, eating the fear when it tried to rise, swallowing it. They would see no trace of it on his stiffening face.

"Tell my son—" He took a deep breath. It was not as easy as he'd imagined it, yearning for this moment in front of a mirror, playing with Death, the razor in his hand. "Tell my son what time his father died. Tell him that I—"

"No!" Mercedes interrupted, pressing his son to her chest. "He won't know your name."

Blood drained from Vidal's face. For the first time in his life he felt terror. This was the moment he'd always dreamt—the one he'd rehearsed in the mirror every morning. Honor in death. This couldn't be going so wrong, it just couldn't. His mind was racing.

Pedro raised his pistol and shot him in the face. The bullet shattered Vidal's cheekbone and severed his optic nerve on the way to his brain. There it lodged in the back of his cranium. The entry wound cried a single tear of blood. Such an insignificant wound, but Death was nesting in it.

With a regretful groan, Vidal collapsed at the feet of the men he had come to hunt. And like that, he was gone.

His son began to cry in Mercedes's arms.

The Boy Who Escaped

Once upon a time, but not long ago, there lived a Child Eater in an ancient forest. The villagers who picked up the deadwood under the trees to get through the winter called him the Pale Man. His victims were so numerous their names covered many walls in the halls he'd built underground, below the forest. He made their bones into furniture as delicate as their limbs, and their screams were the music that accompanied his feasting at the very table on which he'd killed so many of them.

The winding corridors of the Child Eater's lair had been designed to make the chase more enjoyable. Children could be surprisingly fast, as the Pale Man knew. After all he'd been human himself once, but his murders of children had turned him into something else, faceless and ageless, one of his kind.

Cruelty had been his craft since he was a boy. Even then people called him *Pálido*, for he didn't like to be in the sun, so his skin was always as pale as a watery moon. He first practiced on insects, then birds, then his mother's cats.

He killed the first child when he was only thirteen—his younger brother, who he had both loved and envied.

Shortly after that, he went to work for a priest of the Spanish Inquisition, the terrible tool the Catholic Church used to persecute and kill all those who questioned its dogmas. The priest taught Pálido the most intriguing things about torture and numerous methods to kill, and after three years, Pálido's skills had surpassed his master's, so he practiced his skills on him. He consumed the priest's heart while it was still beating, as he'd read that cruelty could be multiplied by devouring it. And indeed, Pálido felt an even more devious darkness after that meal, his own cruelty enhanced by the priest's righteousness and missionary zeal.

One night when he'd outdone himself with a victim, Pálido's own eyes couldn't bear to watch his deeds any longer. They dropped out of their sockets like overripe fruit and the Pale Man carved holes in his own hands so from then on he could wear his eyes in his palms. At times they could prove to be a great hindrance when he was hunting. Three children managed to escape because his eyes failed him. The Pale Man kept two of their names on his walls nevertheless. But the third he erased. It was the name of a scrawny boy, barely six years old, who he'd stolen from a village south of the forest. *Serafín Avendaño.* . . . Although the Pale Man chiseled the name off his walls, he could never forget it.

The Child Eater always used a silver dagger with a gold handle for his murders, an instrument of extraordinary beauty and sharpness that he'd owned for more than three hundred years. It had been a gift from the Grand Inquisitor and he kept it, wrapped in velvet the color of blood, in a locked compartment in the wall of his dining room. The Pale Man had never kept where he stored it a secret from his victims. What for? In the end they were all doomed to die.

Serafín Avendaño had six older brothers who enjoyed to chase him and beat him as their father did them, so the boy had learned from a very young age how to run fast to escape. Serafín had slipped out of the Pale Man's grip as smoothly and swiftly as an eel and, while his captor was reaching for his eyes, the boy had grabbed not only a golden plate filled with food from the bloodstained table, but also the golden key to the compartment in which the Pale Man kept the dagger. It was all Serafín could do for the other captive children who were crying and sobbing in their cages underneath the monster's dining hall.

The corridor Serafín chose to escape seemed endless and soon he heard his captor screaming behind him. At that moment the boy blessed his brothers, whom he had always thought to be the curse of his life, as he streaked past pillars made from bones that lined the corridor. The Pale Man's servants cleaned the tile floors every morning, but they had overlooked a trace of blood. Serafín jumped over it—six years weigh so much less than the 353 years the Child Eater had seen—but the Pale Man slipped in it, and while he was on his knees searching for his eyes, Serafín reached the end of the corridor—and one of the many doors through which the Child Eater made his way in and out of the forest.

The boy stumbled through the door, slamming it behind him, and managed to bar it with a thick branch. Then he ran into the forest, shaking with both terror and relief. Serafín didn't know where he was going. He only knew he had to get away and somehow back to his village and his family.

By the time the boy ran past the mill, where years ago a nobleman's soldiers had drowned a witch, the key he still clutched in his hand felt like a curse. What if it could draw its owner to him? Serafín didn't notice the huge toad watching him when he hurled the key into the pond, nor that it had the eyes of a man. Neither did the boy see the toad swallow the key with its wart-covered lips. (That is another story.)

Serafíín Avendaño escaped that day and, later on, he became an artist who throughout the rest of his life painted images of great beauty to light up the darkness he'd seen as a child.

39

THE RETURN OF THE PRINCESS

Mercedes had never gone all the way into the labyrinth. She'd always feared what she would find and she had been right. She knew it when she saw Ofelia lying by the side of the well.

Mercedes handed Pedro the baby. She would have to forget the baby's father or she wouldn't be able to love the child, and love was what they all needed so desperately. It felt strange that another woman had passed two children into her care. Mercedes prayed she would be able to keep at least her son safe. She for sure had failed her daughter.

When she knelt by Ofelia's side, the pain tearing at her heart was as sharp as if the girl truly were her child. Ofelia was dying. She didn't even have the strength to turn her head to Mercedes, her fading eyes staring blindly at the blood dripping from her hand into the well.

The blood reddened the rainwater at the bottom of the well. The rain had filled the patterns of the labyrinth surrounding the column and the reflection of the moon floated in the shallow water like a ball of silver, the kind of ball fairy-tale princesses lose in a well. The edges of this one, though, were dyed red with Ofelia's blood. Some drops had found their way onto the weathered stone of the column, and crimson flowers were growing from the chiseled image of the girl holding the baby.

Tears running down her face, Mercedes began to hum the lullaby she'd once sung to Ofelia. Softening the girl's laborious breathing, the tune filled the night with memories of innocence, of hope and happiness, and the full moon covered Ofelia with a blanket of silver. She felt its light cool her feverish skin and her aching heart.

Such brilliant light.

"Arise, my daughter," a voice commanded.

Mercedes didn't hear the voice. But Ofelia did.

The moonlight turned into liquid gold, enveloping and caressing her.

It was so easy to rise to her feet. Her limbs, so heavy with Death a moment before, suddenly weighed nothing, and she found herself wearing a coat in lavish crimson and gold. It was sewn from the most precious red silk, as red as blood. And the golden thread pattern on it held fast many precious stones: rubies, emeralds, and opals. Her shoes were red too, and they fit her feet perfectly.

Gone was the aching, gone was the pain, and when she looked around, she saw she was standing in a hall so huge the ceiling seemed almost as far away as the sky. On one wall was a stained-glass window, as round as the full moon, breaking the light into every color of the rainbow, and in front of the window were three magnificent thrones rising high above the golden floor on pillars sculpted like the slender trunks of birch trees.

Ofelia's lips formed a long-lost smile. The woman sitting on the left throne looked very familiar.

"Mother!" she exclaimed. Her tongue had so yearned to speak that word again.

The woman on the throne was holding a baby. *Her brother?*

"*Ofelia.*" The crowned man on the center throne was calling her.

He was wearing a robe that resembled royal robes from her fairy-tale books, but his face was one Ofelia knew—a face that used to lean patiently over a piece of fabric.

"*Father . . . Oh, Father . . .*"

"You have sacrificed your own blood rather than the blood of an innocent," he said with the soft voice Ofelia remembered singing her to sleep before the world became dark. "That was the final task and the most important one." He looked over to his wife.

The mother-queen looked so young and happy. The Fairies were fluttering around her—all three of them, alive!—and from behind the queen's throne stepped the Faun, his body as golden as the walls of the hall. He spread his arms with a welcoming smile as the Fairies swarmed around Ofelia, chattering with excitement.

"And you chose well, Your Highness!" their master exclaimed, bowing his head so deeply his horns almost touched the floor.

"Come here, my daughter!" the queen called, gesturing to the third throne. "Sit by our side. Take your rightful place. Your father has been waiting for you for so long."

In the galleries above them, people rose to their feet. Through their applause, though, Ofelia could still hear Mercedes crying while the blood of the dying girl in her arms was dripping down into the well. She recognized the lullaby Mercedes hummed.

And then . . .

Ofelia smiled—oh so faintly—and then could hear no more.

And Mercedes bent over the dead girl and sobbed until the dark hair was wet with her tears.

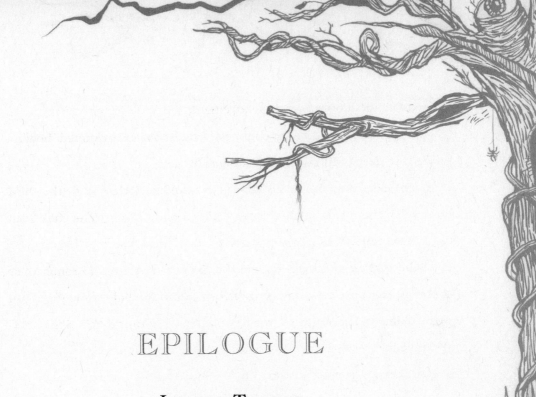

EPILOGUE

LITTLE TRACES

Soon after our story ended, the woods were vacant again. A few years passed and the moss and the earth reclaimed what was left of the mill.

History forgot Vidal, but it also forgot Mercedes, Pedro, Dr. Ferreira, and all the others who sacrificed their own happiness and sometimes their lives to fight fascism. Spain stayed under the regime of Franco for decades and the allies did betray the rebels because they didn't consider them useful allies against their new enemy, the Soviet Union.

As for Ofelia, the morning after she died a small pale flower sprouted on the branch of the old fig tree she had freed from the Toad. It grew in the exact spot where Ofelia had hung her new clothes to keep them safe while she fulfilled the Faun's first task. The petals of the flower were as white as the apron her mother had made for her and at the center of the flower a yellow sun full of pollen and life emerged.

A few years later a poacher came past the burned-down mill and the labyrinth. He couldn't resist stepping through the stone arch and lost himself in the ancient corridors until he was worried he'd never find his way out. But finally the labyrinth led him back to the arch and he felt so tired that he lay down under the fig tree, which by now was in full bloom and festooned with flowers and leaves.

The poacher fell asleep in the gentle shade and in his dreams he heard a story—about a princess birthed by the moon but in love with the sun. He returned to his village and told everyone who listened that the ancient tree had whispered him a story and that it ended in this manner:

And it is said, that the princess Moanna returned to her father's kingdom, and reigned there with justice and a kind heart for many centuries. That she was loved by her people and left behind small traces of her time on earth visible only to those who know where to look.

It's always just a few who know where to look and how to listen, that is true. But for the best stories, a few are just enough.